TEXAS YANKEE

Dan Canby was a Texan—and therefore he was a rebel. He wasn't about to let anybody tell him what to do, including any other Texans.

So Dan didn't fight in the Civil War. He had his own particular war to fight, a tough one, providing food and goods for those left behind—naturally at a profit, because a man has to live.

But when the war was over and the despised Northerners descended on Abilene, and most particularly when a Sergeant of the Union Army started to tell Dan Canby how and when and where he could trade—that was when Dan's mulish, stubborn guts got him into real trouble. Which only went to prove that you can beat a man to his knees but if he's a Texan with a trading Yankee streak—he'll get right back up again.

TEXAS YANKEE

Wade Everett

GUNSMOKE

This hardback edition 2006
by BBC Audiobooks Ltd
by arrangement with
Golden West Literary Agency

ISBN 10: 1 4056 8087 3
ISBN 13: 978 1 405 68087 5

British Library Cataloguing in Publication Data available.

Printed and bound in Great Britain by
Antony Rowe Ltd., Chippenham, Wiltshire

TEXAS YANKEE
Wade Everett

1

As SOON as she heard Hank Swain, Amy Leland put down her pen and closed the ledger over it, then picked up her "swear box" and walked out of the hot freight office. She went across the wagon yard, sidestepping manure piles and muddy spots; Hank Swain was trying to harness a six-up span of mules, and sweat ran off his face and soaked his shirt, and men stood around and watched him.

They watched Amy Leland coming and smiled, and Hank turned as she said, "All those unprintables will cost you a dollar. Pay now."

Swain threw down a mass of harness leather and took off his hat and angrily flogged dust off his clothes. "Now damn it—"

"Careful," she warned. "The price will go up." She was a small woman in her twenties, with a mass of naturally wavy brown hair and blue eyes that could stare right at a man and make him wish he hadn't said that.

"It seems to me with all the trouble—"

She held up her hand, and Hank Swain stopped talking; he dug into his dirty jeans and produced a dollar, dropping it in the box. "That was my last dollar," he said. "Meant to have a drink at Muller's crossin'." He wiped his sleeve across his sweaty face and began to mutter. "Workin' for a woman—it ain't natural, that's what."

"Hank, do you want to quit?"

He pawed a circle in the dirt with his toe. "I went to work for your pa the first day he rolled a wagon, and I guess I'll stay on until they stop—which may not be long, the rate things are goin'."

"And in the meantime we'll learn how to talk without swearing, won't we?" She turned her head quickly and looked at the men standing about. "All caught up with your work?"

They were stirred to instant activity, and she smiled to herself and went back into the hot office. It wasn't much, board and batten, with a tin roof that turned it into an oven by midday. She rattled the swear box and decided to empty it; she took off the lid and dumped the money on her desk and counted it—nearly thirty dollars. She had a tin box in the safe, and she added this money to it and scratched the new total, a little over three hundred dollars, on the torn-out ledger sheet she kept in the box.

That certainly was a lot of swearing, she had to admit to herself. Expecially when it spanned only five months.

She planted her elbows on the desk and put her chin in her hands and looked out the window at the end of the main street, the buildings crowded cheek by jowl, and beyond, the endless rolling plains of Texas, unfenced from the Indian Nations to Matamoros.

It was a land of extremes: dust and wind in the summers and rain and mud in the winter and now and then snow and a bone-aching cold snap. It was the land of the Kiowa and the Comanche and the buffalo, and every man was a law unto himself.

And it was Amy Leland's land, although in five years she had nearly forgotten that.

Nothing in Texas was the same; the war fought a thousand miles away had reached out and changed everything, used up Texas resources and Texas men and Texas money, then left it like some sick and spent thing to gasp out its last breath.

There had been a time when Texas, after defeating Mexico, had grown until it just seemed never to find an end to it. The gulf ports were calls for vessels flying many flags, and Texas beef fattened the South.

Amy Leland could remember well how it was before the war. Largely populated by transplanted Southern men, the ties to Louisiana and Georgia and Alabama and Kentucky were strong; Texas lived and grew and played and never really thought about the North at all, and what trade goods managed to trickle in hardly caused a stir on the market.

Texas was an extension of the South; she carried on an immense trade, and when war was declared, she broke from the Union and gave her young men to the South.

Now it was almost over, and some of the men had already come back, but not to the Texas they had left. The town still stood, and the mansions the cattle barons had built still stood, but they were shells now, lived in but not really alive, for Texas was standing still, strangling because there was no one to trade with now, and the Yankees controlled the seaports with their blockades, and men just didn't know where to turn.

They looked for work, and when there wasn't any, they turned to stealing, from the Yankee Army at first, and when the pickings got lean, they started stealing from one another, and soon the terms "outlaw" and "renegade" didn't mean anything bad; it was just another way of making a living.

A fever had taken her mother in '59, and her father had decided that it was time for her to go East and get an education and marry some fine man who would never once in his life think seriously of going to Texas. She went because it was what he wanted, and a little bit of what she wanted, too, because she had already had eight grades of Abilene's one-teacher, one-room school, and she could play the pump organ and properly set a table; her mother had taught her those things, the commandments of a gentlewoman.

She had felt it was time to go on, to become a lady, and no age is finer than seventeen to begin.

St. Louis was not as fine a town as Boston or Baltimore or even Philadelphia for this purpose, but she had a maiden aunt there who knew a good school, and St. Louis had become Amy Leland's home for five years. A good five years. Not always happy, but not altogether sad, and the prospects of a good marriage were bright; the man was from a good family, big in the tannery and fur business, with a manufacturing branch that made all kinds of leather goods, from small men's clasp purses to harness and saddles and buggy dashboards.

His name was Taylor Blaine and his sympathy Southern, a dashing man of twenty-six, tall, athletic, and inclined to accept credit for things not quite accomplished. Amy Leland was not sure that she loved him, but if not, she had been willing to accept what she felt for love and was sure she could be happily married on it.

But that had never come to pass. Jake Leland, her father, had camped the night near the Peace, on his way to a buffalo hunters' camp near a place that would later be known as Adobe Walls. Sometime during the night a rattlesnake had joined Leland in his blankets. No one knew what happened, really, but Hank Swain figured that maybe Leland rolled on the snake, angered it; anyway, he was bitten, and he died out there on the prairie, bloated and alone, beyond help and hope.

Another freighter found him almost a week later, and since Leland left a will, Amy, aged twenty-two, was summoned from St. Louis and told that she had inherited a freight line, consisting of six heavy wagons, eighty mules, a freight yard, four way stations, and a payroll of thirty some men.

Taylor Blaine and all he represented faded into unimportance once Amy found herself back on home ground. She had a business without competition, but not without trouble; the Indians were a bother, and with the war on, renegades parading as loyal soldiers of the Confederacy stole everything they could get their hands on, and each success made them bolder, more aggressive.

Amy Leland opened the books she had been working on, glanced at the sums, and marveled that she could still be breaking even, let alone showing a little profit. She ran wagons to Austin, connecting there with the railroad, and serviced the towns and Ranger posts in between, a stretch of two hundred miles. And her wagons went north, into the Staked Plains country for the Indian and buffalo hunter trade; that was her profit, and she didn't want to lose it.

She closed the safe and locked it, then left the office and walked down the street to the square and the Mexican quarter beyond. Children and dogs chased each other, unmindful of the heat, and around the well curbing women pounded clothes with wooden paddles while their men slept in the shade.

The Martinez adobe was crowded in among the others, and Pablo Martinez was sleeping by the door; she stirred him gently with her foot, and he came awake, got to his feet when he saw who it was.

He swept off his hat and bowed, and Amy said, "Pablo, would you like work?"

"Sí."

"I want you to build an adobe office for me, and another adobe building for the men to live in."

"Sí, it can be done."

"If you do good work, I'll pay you two hundred dollars."

"I am the best builder in the town," Pablo assured her. "When must I commence?"

"As soon as you can."

He grinned. "It will have thick walls to hold out the heat, and a roof of tile to keep out the rain. You will be pleased, senorita."

"Use the wood from the old buildings for beams and flooring," Amy Leland said. "I'll pay as the work goes along, Pablo. How many weeks will it take?"

He thought a moment. "Three at the most."

"Then I'll pay you a third each week."

He bowed again and smiled, and she turned and made her way through the heat back toward the freight yard. Waves danced from the dust in the street, and the sun bounced off the bleached wooden walls like a blow, making even the shade beneath the porches thick and stuffy.

Dan Canby was standing in his doorway, watching her progress along the street; he spoke as she drew even. "The heat'll get you if you don't wear a hat, Amy."

She stopped and squinted at him; he was a lanky man in a white shirt, with a bone-handled pistol stuck into his belt, butt to the front. He had a bold face and a dark mustache and even darker eyes; they always made her very alert, as though Canby were going to take advantage of her if she didn't watch him closely. He was a soft-spoken man and very dangerous; she had seen him shoot two men not far from the very spot where she stood.

"Do you worry about me?" she asked.

"Why, sure. With only six unmarried females in town, it's like me to worry." He smiled. "Still say you ought to throw your outfit in with mine."

"No. How many times does that make now?"

"Oh, forty or fifty. I never keep track of the noes. Just the yeses." He straightened. "Got some tea inside. I've got a cistern, the best in town, and—"

"Thank you, no."

"I'm not going to bite you," he said.

"Now I didn't say you were." She compressed her lips. "Don't think a dare will work with me, Dan Canby."

"Didn't expect it to." He smiled again. "But I guess it's just your way of flattering yourself."

"What's that supposed to mean?"

"Oh, I don't know how to tell you. But if you were fifty and fat, you'd come in and drink the tea, but since you're young and pretty, you've just got to figure that I'll chase you around the sugar barrels and—"

"Well, I like that!" she snapped and came onto the porch. When she reached the doorway, Canby put out his hand, touching her with his fingertips.

"Hold on now. I want you to know I deliberately boogered you into comin' in. If you don't want to, then don't."

She looked at him a moment then said, "That's honest of you to admit it. Are you always this way?"

"Try to be."

"Then I'll have some tea," she said and walked past him. His store was ten degrees cooler, choked with the flavors of spices and leather and coal oil. His rooms and office were in back, and she went there, and he wound the windlass on the cistern. She watched him, then said, "My, that's a way down, isn't it?"

"Over a hundred feet. Mexicans dug a well here nearly forty years ago. Went dry, so I use it for a cistern. 'Course it's got some water in it now, but it keeps things nice and cold." The hopper came up, and he poured from a glass jug.

Immediately her glass began to sweat, and she drank some of the tea. "My, that is good. Really cold."

"The best cistern in town," he admitted, sitting on the edge of the kitchen table. "How's business?"

"Well, still holding its own." She regarded him seriously. "May I ask you a question?"

"Sure."

"When Dad died, quite a few men in town came to me with bills that he owed them. I've been waiting for you to show up."

"He didn't owe me anything," Dan Canby said evenly. "Fact is, I owed him eighty dollars for some freight haulin'. I'd like to pay it now. You can give me a receipt when you get around to it."

"Why didn't you say something before?"

"What good would it have done? I didn't have the money. I do a lot of business on a swap basis, Amy. Besides, Confederate dollars just ain't as popular with some of those New Orleans merchants as Yankee gold. I'm payin' you in gold."

"I'd take Confederate money, Dan."

He shook his head. "Made the deal with your pa for Yankee gold, and that's what I'll pay." He got up and crossed to his desk and took the money out of the cashbox and counted it out for her. "It ain't my way to stick my nose in someone else's business, but I don't recollect your pa ever owing Pete Field and Doc Scully anything."

"How would you know?"

Canby shrugged his thin shoulders. "I hear 'most everything that goes on in Abilene, Amy. I just never heard about that."

"Well, I paid them, a total of four hundred dollars. And more than I could afford," she added.

"Scully never sold your pa any mules. Field never had a lien on the wagons, either."

She compressed her lips tightly. "That makes me look like a fool, doesn't it? I suppose everyone has been laughing at me?"

"Well, they were at the start," Canby said, "but they've learned a bit different. You've lasted."

"And what did you think?"

"Honestly?"

"Of course. I don't cry easily."

"Yeah, so I've learned. Well, I didn't think you'd last.

Most of us figured you'd sell out and go back to St. Louis. Now it seemed natural, didn't it? We heard you had a man back there you was thinking of marrying." He smiled, and he had a very pleasant face. "I'm happy to be wrong, though."

"Dan, are you positive about Scully and Field?"

He nodded. "Absolutely. However, it's not been my place to say or do anything, Amy. You'd have resented it, and—"

"That's right, I would have. Dan, will you lend me a pistol?" He started to take his .44 cap-and-ball Remington from his belt, but she shook her head. "I'd never be able to cock that."

"Come on," he said and went into his store, taking her behind the counter to a glass showcase of pistols. He took a .36 Remington pocket revolver out of the case, loaded it, seated caps on the nipples, and handed it to her.

"How much is this pistol?"

"Twenty-one dollars. Why don't you just take the loan of it?" He watched her steadily, and then she nodded and turned to the front door. When she left his porch, he stood in the doorway, watching her cross over and walk down a block to where Pete Field had his blacksmith shop.

Field was folding some red-hot strap iron over a round mandrel, making hinges, and he looked up with some surprise when Amy Leland stopped in his doorway. Field was a man of tremendous girth, but he had strength to go along with his beef, and some said that he had shod oxen, double shoe, without using a yoke and stall.

He saw the pistol and stood there, hammer hanging loose in his hand. "What you want, Miss Leland?"

"The money you said my father owed you," Amy said. "You were lying."

"I don't allow a man to say that to me, and I like it no less when a woman says it." He raised his hammer to go on working, then stopped when she cocked the pistol. "Put that away now."

"I paid you two hundred and nine dollars. Get it for me now."

Pete Field tipped his head back and laughed, then he let the humor vanish and looked past her. "Did you tell her this, Canby?"

Amy shot a glance behind her; Canby was leaning against

one of the support poles, and she saw that he was not carrying his gun. "I wouldn't lie to her, Pete. And I figure it was a mistake for you to."

"Now I see it," Field said. "You've come along to see that she gets it back."

"Nope. I came to watch her get it back." He slapped his plank of a stomach. "No gun, Pete. However, she's got one." He smiled and lit a cigar.

"I'm not scared of a woman," Pete Field said and dropped his hammer on his work. Amy Leland fired, bouncing the bullet off the anvil, making it ring and startling Field enough so that he dropped back a step. Powder smoke drifted in the still air, and he looked at Amy Leland, his mouth slack.

"I'll take what you owe me now," she said.

Field hesitated, and Dan Canby said, "Was I you, I'd get it, Pete."

Field kept his money in a leather sack, hidden in a stall, in a grain box, and he counted it out, dropping the gold pieces into her palm, slowly, as though they were drops of blood from his own veins. Then he looked at Dan Canby. "I figure you owe me this now, Dan."

"You figure wrong, but if you're a mind to collect, you know where I'll be." He turned then and walked back to his store and went inside.

Amy Leland stepped out of the blacksmith shop and cut across the street to where Doe Scully had a livery stable and corral. Scully had been standing in his doorway, and from the expression on his face, Amy Leland guessed that he had heard it all.

"I didn't mean no real harm," he said when she came up. He worked his jaws furiously on some burley twist and watched her with unwavering attention. "I sure don't want any trouble over this, Miss Leland."

"Just what do you think you have now?" she said. "You're a crook, Doe Scully, and everyone in town's going to know about it. Now get the money you weaseled out of me."

"Sure thing now." He bowed and grinned and ducked inside. She heard a door slam shut; he had quarters in a shack on one side of the barn, and she supposed he had gone there. Then she heard Scully yelp, and there was a heavy clatter of something falling; a moment later Scully came out, the money in his hand. A dribble of blood ran from the corner of his mouth, mingling with the tobacco juice in his beard.

"Fell," he said and gave her the money. "No hard feelin's, be there?"

"What do you think?"

She turned and walked back toward Dan Canby's store; he was inside, standing behind the counter, sorting through some sacked goods. She laid the pistol on the counter. "How much for firing it once?"

"Oh, I don't think it hurt it much," Canby said. "I'll clean it, and it'll be as good as new." He reached for the pistol, and she saw that he had two knuckles skinned.

Quickly she put out her hand, over his. "All right, honest man, how did it happen?" She looked at him, then smiled. "You went in the back way, didn't you? What was he going to do, Dan?"

"Well, he had some foolish idea. There wasn't time to talk him out of it, so—"

"—so you hit him in the mouth."

He grinned and ran his fingers through his hair. "Yeah, somethin' like that. You can keep on holding my hand if you like, though."

She pulled hers away quickly and put it behind her. "I'm not going to thank you."

"Didn't expect it."

"Then why'd you do it?"

He shrugged. "Scully's a mean old cuss. Maybe a little more than I wanted to see you handle. Fact is, you'd have had to shoot him, and I didn't want to see you do that. Too nice a day."

"Dan, I've got to take care of my own affairs."

"Sure you do."

She studied him, trying to understand him, then she turned and stepped to the door. "You've bought trouble for yourself, Dan."

"Well, it was so cheap I just couldn't turn it down. That's the bargain hunter in me."

"Then thank you."

He watched her go, then dropped the loading lever, pulled

the cylinder pin, and let the cylinder fall free. He pulled the loads with a corkscrew, cleaned the gun thoroughly, reassembled it, and returned it to the display case.

Pete Field and Doc Scully came in, stopping just inside the door. Scully carried a Sharps rifle, and Field had a .36 Colt jammed in the waistband of his leather apron.

"You shouldn't have stuck your nose in," Scully said. "It wasn't any business of yours anyway, Dan."

"Oh, I don't know; it never did set right with me." He looked from one to the other. "You want a little trouble over it?"

"You must have figured you had that when you told her," Field said. "That was the first hard money I'd seen in a year, Dan. Damn it all!"

"Cheatin' a woman—is that the way to get it?" Canby asked.

"What do you get out of this?" Scully asked. "Or don't you want me to guess?"

"I'd advise you not to," Canby told him. He walked down the length of the counter and came around the end, and then they saw the sawed-off eight-gauge Greener with the hammers eared back. He placed the shotgun on the counter but kept his fingers curled around the stock, and both men looked at it. "The trouble with both of you is that you're sore losers. Jake Leland wouldn't take you in as a partner, not even when he needed one. He had you figured out, Scully—a dirty little man with a big ambition and nothing else." He switched his glance to Pete Field. "You never put a shoe on Leland stock, and that galled you bad. And you never could beat Jake to anything, so you decided to take it out on the girl. That was a mistake."

"Who says so?"

"She does."

"She's just a woman," Field said. "If she was a man—"

Canby laughed. "Pete, if she was a man, you'd never have had the guts to cheat her."

Field thought about this, then said, "Are you throwin' in with her, Dan?"

He shook his head. "She won't have it."

"A man like you never picks up an ax unless he means to grind it," Scully said. "Known you too long to think otherwise. Maybe you want a part of that line. Never knew you to mix in another's fuss before."

"You learn somethin' new every day, don't you?"

"Yeah, and some things a man don't forget," Field declared.

"But I'll wait. I've got the time." He wheeled and stomped out, knocking back a man who was standing out there, listening to it all.

"Now how about you?" Dan Canby asked. "Ain't you goin' to threaten me and leave?"

"I don't figure it's worth shootin' over," Scully said. "She can't last. She's a woman. She just can't last. Ain't tough enough."

"Now you'd be a fool to bet on that, Doc."

Scully scratched his head and turned to spit; he splattered the boots of a man standing just outside the door; there was a good crowd now, and the man had no chance to jump back. This angered Scully, and he snapped, "What the hell you all want? Go on, get out of here!"

"You go," Canby said easily, and Scully's head came around quickly.

"Don't talk to me that way, Dan. You want to lose a friend —"

"You were never a friend of mine," Canby told him.

Scully hesitated. "Can't figure it. I just can't figure your game at all."

"Well, you work on it then." He stood there, and Scully turned and pushed his way through the men standing around the porch. They hesitated a moment and then moved on, and Dan Canby put the shotgun behind the counter and stood there, frowning a little.

It seemed odd to him that men like Scully and Field couldn't understand that a man did things just because they were the right things to do. Then he wondered if maybe they weren't a little right about him—that there was something behind it that he really didn't understand himself.

2

AUGUST was the hottest month anyone remembered, and through the ceaseless, blistering heat Pablo Martinez and four of his relatives labored to build the two buildings Amy Leland wanted. Martinez was a craftsman; he laid his blocks true and vertical, and each window and door was square, with the heavy timbers mortised into the adobe.

A saw pit was built, and the timbers of the old buildings were ripped for planks, and each one was carefully smoothed and oiled, then laid down, drilled and pegged in place. Martinez, who had a reputation for being a listless, idle man, worked from the first peek of the morning sun to the last view of it, and he completed the buildings in twenty-six days, took the last of his money, and went home.

The next day he resumed his siestas while his wife beat clothes at the well.

Hank Swain was summoned to the office, and Amy Leland laid down a few ground rules. There would be no spitting of tobacco on the floor, and because she knew the contrary nature of these men, she added the walls and ceiling to that rule. The barracks would be scrubbed once a week, each Saturday, and she would inspect it personally. The bathing facilities—a large metal tank installed at the west end—would be used frequently.

And any man who didn't like it could draw his pay and leave.

Hank Swain didn't like it, but he chewed his tobacco and

17

nodded, and because the only kind of job he knew how to do was a good one, the orders would be followed to the letter.

Mail was delivered by Amy Leland's drivers. That is, it was brought to Dan Canby's store, and people picked it up there when they came to town, and it was not unusual for letters and packages to go uncalled for for a month or more.

But any news of the war spread quickly because many of these people had kin fighting in the South; the country had almost been denuded of young men, some of them away for their third year now, and many had gone for good, fallen or died in Yankee prisons.

The war wasn't going well, and ideas of an early victory had vanished. No one said that the South was losing; they just stopped talking about the South winning, especially after the siege of Vicksburg. Once in a while men would come back, some riding, some walking, some with an empty sleeve or an eye gone; they went to their homes and stayed there as though they were hiding from something, and a few of them joined the renegades, thinking they could go on fighting that way.

The rains began in the early fall, heavy showers that soaked the land and swelled the creeks, and the buffalo hunting season came to an end, and Amy Leland put all her wagons on the southern run. Somehow the summer had been a good one; she bought four wagons from a man in Santa Fe who wanted out of the business, and she took thirty of his mules and six men he had working for him. It seemed incredible, but she paid cash, nearly eleven hundred dollars for the lot, delivered.

By careful management she was showing a profit, looking for every opportunity to put her hands on Yankee gold, and when she took Confederate money, she insisted that it be discounted, at first only ten percent, then later twenty, and now she'd only accept it at fifty cents on the dollar.

There was a lot of talk about this; some said that she was downright unpatriotic and that a body ought to have more faith in Jefferson Davis, but that was street talk. The merchants were shying away from Confederate money and more often would accept script, privately printed paper that in reality was only promissory notes backed by the large landowners and cattlemen.

Dan Canby came to her office one evening; it was early, but the sun was down, and she was working on the records by lamplight. He knocked, then stepped inside and unbuttoned his coat.

"Got a few minutes?"

"Well, since you're one of my biggest accounts, I guess I have. Sit down." She saw that he carried an unlighted cigar between his fingers. "Smoke if you like. Ordinarily I wouldn't allow it, but since you pay your bills on time——"

"I knew there was some reward in virtue," Canby said and scratched a match on the sole of his boot. "Thought we'd have a little talk about the business world and the way things are going."

She swiveled her chair and looked at him. "Talk. I'm listening."

"Well, as a practical man, I'd say it was just a matter of time before the South turns belly up. Not a pretty thing to say, but a man has to be smart enough to know when he's been licked. Agree?"

"I don't disagree."

"Looking at the whole situation from a business standpoint, things could be a lot better, and they could be one hell of a lot worse. The Yankee blockade of Texas ports two years ago was nothing at all. You could either buy your way clear or slip by; they just didn't have the picket ships to do a good job of it. Last year it was some different. Things began to tighten up, and getting through to New Orleans was a tough job." He rolled his cigar around in his mouth. "Right now you'd be lucky if you could sneak a rowboat through, the ports are so well blockaded. So there's no use in talking about doing business with New Orleans. Money is tight, and Confederate paper just isn't worth much; they want Yankee gold or nothing, and I don't blame them."

"What's your point, Dan?"

"That things are going to get worse before they get better. You and me, we may be out of business before this is over. Hate to see that. A lot of hard work going for nothing." He took a letter from his coat pocket and laid it on her desk. "The way I see it, we're just running out of everything—money, something to sell, and a place to sell it. Confederate goods are poor quality; everyone's in a hurry or short of this or that. Yankee goods will bring top dollar. They'll bring gold out of cookie jars and burial places, gold that's been saved for real tough times." He put his hand on the letter. "About eight months ago I sent a letter overland to a friend of mine in California, telling him to be on the lookout for something good to buy. Well, I got this in the last mail. He owned several stores in the gold country. Now he wants to sell out. The price is so good I can't afford to pass it up."

"Keep talking," Amy invited.

"I'm talking about all Yankee goods, Amy. First-class quality. Goods like Texas hasn't seen in three years. Wool blankets that will last fifteen years, and cotton shirts with real buttons, not wooden ones. Can you imagine it? Jeans with real copper rivets, and knives and forks that aren't tinplate?"

"If the stuff's so good, how come he can't sell it there?"

"The gold petered out, and the whole town, about fifteen thousand people, just packed up and took off."

"I was talking about San Francisco."

"San Francisco is glutted with hard goods, and the market's down. He can't give the stuff away there. That's why it's a good buy for me. I can get it at a price that's more than he could sell for in San Francisco, yet a lot less than he paid for it. He just wants to take as small a loss as possible."

"California's a long way, Dan. I take it you're asking me to haul for you?"

"Yes, if you'll go for the deal."

"How many wagons?"

"Twenty-five or more."

She laughed. "You know I don't have—"

"Better listen to the deal. Ore wagons are going begging; I can pick them up in California. Oxen, too."

"Now I don't want oxen."

"They're slow, but they're steady."

"My men won't drive them, and I won't ask them to."

"Mexicans will," Canby said. "Amy, I've got it all worked out. I'll take the men with me, and we'll go west and on up through Arizona—the Mexicans have been using those trails for years."

"A lot of miles, Dan. With wagons and oxen?" She shook her head.

"It can be done. And no blockade, either."

"There must be Yankee Army—"

"We'll have to duck the Army. It's a chance I'm willing to take."

"It's a big gamble," she said. "Dan, you could lose your shirt."

"If I sit here doing nothing, I'm going to lose it anyway. So are you. I can swing the whole deal for about four thousand in gold, but I don't have that much. Three thousand is my limit. I need to hire men, get them there, buy wagons and stock and the merchandise, and get back. It'll take seven months on the inside, and I'll need another two thousand."

"You're asking me for two thousand?"

"Yes."

"And what am I getting for my money?"

"Wagons and stock. All right, so you don't like oxen. Then sell them to the Mexicans and get back part of your investment. But these ore wagons will haul three times what your freight wagons carry. And they're built to last."

"There are a lot of gopher holes in this, Dan. You could stumble and break both legs in a dozen places."

"Sure, but it's do it or curl up your toes, and I don't want to do that. People have crossed the desert before, and they'll do it again. I figure it's a fighting chance, and I mean to take it."

"Why come to me?"

He shrugged and gnawed on his cigar. "Well, I've always held to the notion that one of these days you'd stop saying no to me and then we'd kind of merge everything. You've never really pushed me away, you know."

"That sounded almost like a proposal."

"It was. Although when a man's back is against the wall, it's a poor time to think of it. Keep it in mind, though."

"Why, of course. Who'll head this up, Dan?"

"I will if you'll run my store."

When she opened her mouth to object, he held up his hand. "It's just like any other business—profit and loss, and you understand that well enough." He put his cigar aside and leaned forward, his manner intense. "The Yankees let one passenger packet leave Galveston every fifteen days, and I could be on that with men and horses. We'd leave the packet at Vera Cruz, and then it's a four-day ride to a village on the coast called Acapulco. The Mexicans tell me it's no trouble at all to get a schooner to California from there."

"Is there a trail through there?"

"A good road, the way I hear it."

She thought a moment, tapping the pencil against her front teeth. "You know, Dan, it might not be a bad idea to ship south out of San Francisco. You figure the cost of men and animals for five months on the trail, and it comes to a big hunk. Before I really made up my mind to come back overland, I'd look into the availability of shipping."

"A good point. Still, there's the Yankee pickets." He mulled this over. "Of course, it might be possible to go northeast through Mexico and cross the Rio Grande. I don't think that's ever been done, though. The trail down through New Mexico is open; some goods have come in that way. I was just trying to eliminate as many of the risks as possible."

"It wouldn't be very funny to be stopped by a picket boat," Amy said.

"Mmm. No. That would be losing the hard way. I'll look into the shipping angle very carefully. And I suppose we can reduce the time by a good two and a half months this way."

"As well as eliminating Indian trouble. When did you want to start, Dan?"

"In the morning. I can get the men together and—"

"Then I'll have the money for you," she said. "Want to shake on it?"

"I kind of thought a kiss would—"

"Why, how nice of you to think of it," she said and stood up. He put his arms around her, looked at her for a moment, then kissed her, holding her against him for several minutes.

When he released her, she blew out a breath and laughed nervously. "Mr. Canby, that wasn't exactly a decent kiss."

"Want me to take it back?"

Dan Canby was too smart to leave town in the company of sixty Mexican drovers; he made his arrangements with them, and they left in twos and threes, and they met ten days later in Galveston, and there Canby secured passage on the packet *Argonaut*, destination Vera Cruz.

There was some talk around town about the way Amy Leland took over Canby's store. She got wind of it, pinned most of it to Doe Scully, and then took a new buggy whip out of the rack and danced Scully the length of the main street, cutting his legs and backside pretty badly in the process.

The talk stopped, and Scully ate his meals standing for ten days, and Pete Field, not wanting a taste of this, stayed close to his blacksmith shop, industriously pounding away.

Vera Cruz was not what Dan Canby expected; he'd thought it would be a hamlet in the sun, and he was surprised to find a hustling, busy port backed by a large town. As an American, particularly a Texan, he was viewed with a certain suspicion, but the Mexicans with him allayed the fears of the government officials, and they were given a travel permit and left the town without further delay.

The road was not bad; it cut its way through dense rain forest, thick undergrowth with a steaming humidity and bright birds wheeling and hawking and so many snakes that a man had to be very careful where he put down his bedding.

Rain in Canby's part of Texas was rare enough to draw considerable comment, but during the nine-day journey it rained each afternoon near enough to two o'clock for a man to tell time by it. And this was a special rain, with huge, fat drops, pelting down as though merely falling were not good enough. It thundered down, beating foliage, soaking them in seconds, falling so thickly that visibility was actually reduced. It would rain so for fifteen minutes, then abruptly cease, as though someone had turned it off. And then the heat would close in again, and the insects would bite furiously, and the land would steam and smolder and soak up the rain.

Acapulco was a small town crowded against the bluest of seas and sheltered by a crescent bay and a white sandy beach. Fishing boats snuggled against the shore, and in the roads, riding to anchor, a barkentine and a full-rigged ship waited for cargo or passengers.

Canby asked questions and found that the full-rigged ship had put in for repairs and was going around the Horn, destination Liverpool and the River Clyde. The barkentine was plying coastal trade—hides, hard goods, wines, and some passengers. The captain was an Australian, and he agreed on a price to sail with the next tide to San Francisco.

Canby brought his Mexicans and horses aboard, and before sunset the anchor was catted, sail set, and the barkentine heeled to a fresh breeze.

For six days they westered offshore, then the captain tacked about and set a northeasterly course. The weather was balmy with a good trade wind husking them along on the port tack, and Canby, who had never been to sea before, began to enjoy it, and he began to think that Amy was right—that this was better than shipping overland.

That kind of trip was always dangerous, for the Indians were troublesome and unpredictable, and he had never heard of a train getting through without some kind of attack. And there were renegades about who robbed anyone, and the desert was a menace, with water holes few and far between.

She was right; a ship was the fastest and safest way to bring back the goods.

When they sailed through the Golden Gate and passed under the cannon of the Yankee fort, Canby expected trouble from officials and was surprised to find none at all. An officious major asked him his name and destination; Canby told him, and then the major suggested one of the river steamers to Sacramento, even going so far as to point out the pier where the steamers berthed.

With his Mexicans in tow, Canby bought passage, and since there were no cabin accommodations for the Mexicans, Canby slept on deck with them. It was a pleasurable voyage in sheltered waters. Sacramento was a clapboard city with dusty streets and shady trees and a river bank that reminded Canby of the Mississippi and Louisiana. With their horses unloaded, Canby bought supplies and listened to the talk in the stores. All the merchants complained about how poor business was. The gold rush was over in California, and Nevada was getting it now; there had been quite a few silver strikes of late, and the population was migrating there.

Because they were all Yankees, Dan Canby paid particular attention to the people of Sacramento; it was a large town, populated now by farmers and merchants and fruit growers; the get-rich-in-a-hurry population had eased on. Canby was amazed to see a large police force and nice homes with watered lawns and a large section of the town almost totally Chinese.

Canby stayed at the Metropolitan Hotel on West I Street, and it cost him four dollars a day, but the room was splendid luxury and certainly as fine as any hotel in New Orleans. He had sent messages with the Hangtown stage driver to be given to his friend, and four days later Ken Buckley called at the desk, then went up to Canby's room.

They embraced and pounded each other on the back and poured drinks. Canby studied his friend and decided that ten years had brought a few changes. Buckley was tall and heavy through the shoulders, and he wore rough trail clothes, but he carried himself like a man of means.

"Why don't you come back to Texas with me?" Canby suggested.

Buckley laughed and shook his head. "Don't want to sound unkind, Dan, but California's got it all over Texas."

"They're all Yankees!"

"That's a matter of politics," Buckley said, "and a man must learn to live with politics." He sat down and flung an arm over the back of the chair. "So you're in the store business. Well, everyone's got to eat, don't they? I'm moving out of it. To me it was only an investment, and I made my poke. San Francisco's the place for me."

"Got something lined up?"

"Banking," Buckley said casually.

Dan Canby whistled softly. "Say, that appeals to me, but it takes a lot of money."

"I'm going into partnership," Buckley said. "The three of us are putting up half a million."

Canby couldn't help staring; he even swallowed hard. "Ken, you're just not joshing, are you? Half a million dollars? Gold?"

"Gold," Buckley said. "Rather simple. I gambled and made a stake, then moved into the gold fields when the rush started. Poker seemed the best way to make steady money, and I started buying up fractions for whatever small amount I had to pay—sometimes as low as thirty dollars."

"What's a fraction?"

"Odd bits and pieces left over from adjoining claims." He smiled. "I made enough off these pieces to put me into the store business. Had four places until the die-up came. I could sell anything I could get my hands on."

"And I came to buy everything I can get my hands on," Canby said. "When could we get started? I've got sixty Mexicans put up down in Chinee Town. I'm after wagons, mules, horses, oxen, and enough to load the wagons."

"No trouble there except for mules and horses. If a mule can stand, it's worth three hundred dollars. A horse will bring up to seven-fifty. Most of them have been taken over to Nevada. Ranchers around here have stock, but they won't sell. Oxen you can still buy, just like I said in my letter."

"You want to bunk here tonight?"

"I was hoping you'd ask," Buckley said. "And I trust you're treating me to dinner?"

They were enjoying cigars and coffee and brandy, and Buckley had his vest open, indicating that he couldn't hold another bite. "The war," he was saying, "hasn't concerned California much, except to make her rich. I don't suppose there's a businessman out here who hasn't sold Northern goods in Southern markets, with Texas getting a fair share of it. There are outfits freighting to Arizona and New Mexico on a regular basis, and of course from there it gets to Texas, and if you can get past the blockade, some of it finds its way to the Southern states. That's why I wrote you, Dan. I can't sell out here. First off, I'd have to move it all to Nevada or ship it back to San Francisco, and the market just isn't there."

"I thought things were booming."

"The wholesale market isn't," Buckley said. "Besides, I've got to move on this banking venture. There's a lot of talk about building a railroad into Nevada and Utah, and I want in on that. Time is of value to me." He stopped talking and looked past Dan Canby as a big, round-bellied man came up to the table. "Hello, Carver. Do you smell blood?"

The man laughed and sat down. "I smell horses." He offered Canby his hand. "Carver's the name. Do you want to sell your horses?" His glance touched Buckley. "Or have you already bought them?"

Buckley shook his head. "I'm selling, not buying. Besides, I don't have time to drive horses to Nevada and make my profit."

"Heard you were thinking about banking," Carver said. He scratched his muttonchops. "I'm a man of few words, Mr. Canby—I got your name from the clerk. I want to buy your horses, cash, in gold. Five hundred dollars a head, if they're sound."

"Sixty head?" Canby said. "That's thirty thousand dollars."

"I won't mince words," Carver admitted. "I run a stage line, fast mail between San Francisco and the Nevada diggings. I need horses. Good horses. And I'll pay cash."

"Well, I have business in Whiskey Flat," Canby said, "and I don't relish the idea of walking there."

"Understand you've got Mexicans with you, so I'll bend a little. Give me possession of the horses in Whiskey Flat, and I'll pay you then." He sat there, waiting, his heavy watch fob stirring with his breathing.

Finally Canby said, "All right, you've made a deal."

"A pleasure," Carver said, shaking hands. He got up. "Sorry to have disturbed your dinner. I'll see you in Whiskey Flat in—"

"Three days," Buckley said. "We're leaving in the morning."

"That's fine with me," Carver said and left the dining room.

Canby watched him leave, then looked at Buckley. "Did I make a mistake?"

"No more than I'm making selling out my stores. You could take the horses to Nevada and get nearly twice that for them, but it's the bother of doing it, especially when a man's in a hurry to do something else. We've each got to pick our own pie and eat it and let the other fellow have his. No, I'd say you made a good deal."

"And I can get oxen?"

"Oxen you can get," Buckley said, rising. "I'm for an early start. How about you?"

They left at dawn the next day, the entourage of Mexicans strung out behind them, and Canby was amused because they had collected a following of tearful sweethearts in the short time they had been in town.

From the flatlands of the Sacramento Valley they rode through scrub timber and wild olive trees, climbing gently toward the blue-veiled mountains that loomed many miles ahead. The road was well traveled, a good road, and they saw stages going both ways, the drivers whipping along, raising thick clouds of dust.

In two days they reached Dutchman's Flat and found a half dozen people remaining in a town built to house four thousand. The buildings stood empty, some locked, some boarded up, but the majority left open. Canby wanted to see this because he couldn't believe that people would go away and leave furniture and merchandise on the shelves. A lot of it had been looted by travelers, but enough remained to convince him that the owners had just up and left in a hurry.

"What a waste," he told Buckley, who just shrugged.

"You look at these buildings," Buckley said, "and you can see that they're good buildings with only one thing wrong with them."

"What's that?"

"They're in the wrong place."

"But to leave everything—"

"No way to take it along," Buckley said.

Canby was attracted by some abandoned wagons and four mudwagon stages. He and Buckley asked around and could find no one who claimed them, so Canby had horses hitched to the rigs, and they left town.

"It would bother me," Canby said as they moved along the road, "to see a town die like that."

"Depends on what you want. These people were after gold. The town meant nothing to them." He paused to light a cigar. "Someday, when people start farming this land, the town may come alive again. Who knows, and, I guess, who cares?"

"I'd care," Canby said. "I've got to be building, Ken. Growing is what a man does best. Someday I'm going to look back and see the things I've built. That's what I want."

"Do you care how you get there?"

"I'd step on a man if I had to," Canby said frankly.

Columbia was their destination, a substantial town with brick buildings and shady streets, and they, too, were empty now except for a few people who stayed behind because they had small farms or garden patches.

The arrival of the Mexicans caused a stir, but it was short-lived. Buckley's store was in the middle of the block, and they went inside. Dust lay thick on the counters, and Canby stopped and stared at the jungle vine of hanging harness and the shelves bowed under the weight of clothing and hardware.

One wall was covered with canned goods, and he examined them, reading the labels: peaches and apples and tomatoes and potatoes.

"About a hundred cases in all," Buckley said. "My office is in the back room, and I've got a complete inventory there. I have another store in Angel's Camp and one in Murphy's Flat. There was another in Whiskey Flat, but it's not worth bothering with."

"It is to me," Canby said, turning around again to look at the merchandise. "Can I find enough wagons? You wrote about ore wagons."

"They'll be pretty heavy on the Arizona trail," Buckley said. "You see, that's the rub, Dan, getting this stuff overland to Texas. Hell, it'll be winter before you make it back, and with the Indians—"

"I'll take it to San Francisco and ship it and cross Mexico," Canby said. "I've already made the arrangements."

"Can you do that?"

"I've got a better chance than overland. Now how about the ore wagons?"

"Hell, take anything you can find, in that case."

Carver arrived and bought the horses; he had ten men with him, and by late afternoon he had left with the herd, and Canby had three leather pouches of gold coin. The Mexicans were sent out to buy oxen; they were excellent judges of these animals, and in the four days that Canby remained in the town, the old stage corral was gradually filled with these slow, lolling beasts.

Buckley was a little irritated with Canby's methodical, planned manner, but each item was inventoried, accounted for, crated if fragile, and loaded onto a mounting string of ore wagons. Canby stripped the deserted blacksmith shop of shoes and nails and ironware; he knew that when he got back to Abilene, there wouldn't be any of the double shoes for oxen, and he didn't want to lose the battle for survival for want of a nail.

Canby bought out Buckley clean, even to the counters and glass showcases; these he stuffed with cloth and then crated so that the curved glass wouldn't be broken. The wagons were not merely loaded. Each load was precisely packed; then, with lumber taken from buildings, the load was sealed with a stout lid and the entire wagon box fastened with strap iron. When they reached the ship, it was Canby's intention to remove the loaded boxes from the wagon running gear and let them serve as their own containers.

Because Buckley was in a hurry, Mexicans and wagons were dispatched to Angel's Camp and Murphy's Flat and the contents of both stores brought back, there to be inventoried, crated, and put aside. Buckley and Canby haggled a bit over the price, and since Canby was getting a lot more than he had originally planned, he paid Buckley six thousand in gold, and Buckley left, leaving Canby to finish up by himself.

Canby, realizing that few Mexicans ever had enough money to buy firearms, opened two crates of double-barreled shotguns and gave one to each man, along with two boxes of brass shells. As he did this, he realized that the shotguns would have brought a good price in Texas, but he had seven cases of Sharps rifles and two cases of Remington pistols, along with powder, caps, and accouterments already packed and sealed in one wagon.

Each wagon had a code painted on all four sides, and from Canby's records he could instantly tell the contents of the wagon. His original intention had been to take perhaps thirty wagons; he had figured two men to a wagon, but the opportunity to increase this was too great, and finally he had them all loaded—sixty wagons.

It felt good to be ready to move, to pull out, yet he was a long way from Texas, and in Canby's mind there lurked the suspicion that since things had been going so well, they were due for a bad turn. He didn't know what it would be—weather, or something man dreamed up—but he was determined to be ready for it.

They left at dawn, taking the road back, and the oxen made a steady one mile an hour, which gave them about ten hours on the road, for darkness was coming a little earlier each day—not much, just a couple of minutes, but enough so a man could notice.

Each night he posted a heavy guard and kept fires burning, and he slept lightly, a pair of pistols always handy, but the trouble he watched for didn't show up, and in time he made Sacramento.

The wagons were taken to the river, and by nightfall they crowded the deck of a steamer for the journey to San Francisco. The desire to spend a few days in the hotel, sleeping in a good bed, was strong, but the desire to get moving again, to get back to Texas, was stronger, and Canby started down river late that night.

This California, Canby decided, was a wonderful place, and a man could get rich if he had a lick of sense and knew what to do with a dollar. He supposed that Ken Buckley would be worth a million dollars someday, yet the thought of all that money was not lure enough to woo Dan Canby away from Texas.

I'd rather be broke in Texas than rich here, he thought, and knew that this was the truth. He supposed that a man never really analyzed why he felt this way about a place, but the feeling was there, pure and strong, and he sure wouldn't fight it.

San Francisco was an irritation to Canby because he had to delay six days. The barkentine was up river, anchored off Benicia in one of the coves because the water was fresh there and lying to in it killed the barnacles. This was just one of those little details of seamanship that had to be attended to, and once the barnacles were dead, the ship was heeled on the mudflats, and at low tide the sailors scraped her clean.

In time, and on the captain's schedule, the barkentine arrived in San Francisco, and the process of loading began. The wagons were dismantled and loaded in the hold, and Canby was Buckley's guest at one of the fashionable hotels. Delays seemed endless, and this irritated Canby, yet he realized that as Buckley's friend he was making contacts for future business deals, and he was certain there would be more.

Canby was an opportunist in a land of opportunity; he didn't deny this or pretend to be anything else, and neither did Ken Buckley or any of his friends. They were a pleasant group of men who often found themselves jumping at the same chance and bumping heads, and once in a while they pulled some very sharp deals on each other, but they never took it personally.

The world was, they seemed to think, a prize, up for grabs to the man with the quickest hands, and Canby had to go along with that. He talked a lot about Texas, and while none of these men denied that opportunity was there, they didn't want to get involved because of the North-South political difference. Politics, Canby came to learn, was not conducive to good business. When politics entered, profit fled.

To make money, stay out of politics; he swore he would remember that.

Amy Leland received no word from Dan Canby and expected none; mail service was sketchy at best. It either came through the south or was brought in when the Army took a patrol south through the Indian Nations, and the war had put a stop to that.

Her days were spent at the store, and much as she admired Canby's business sense, she felt that there were a lot of things that he didn't stock and should have. It was a man's store, and other than food, there was nothing that appealed to women.

Goods of any kind were increasingly hard to get.

Hank Swain, who managed her freight line now, brought back word from Austin that the State of Texas was offering a mail contract in the spring, with a provision that a coach would arrive and depart each week from the capital. It was a plum, although the pay was in Confederate money. But this wasn't what Amy Leland was interested in; she found the prospect of getting mules and property for way stations very inviting, and the franchise itself was worth something, for it gave a foothold against competitors.

But she had no coaches and no prospect of getting any, while Scully and Field were busy working in a locked barn, building coaches. It made her sick to think of it and to hear Field at the anvil late at night.

Still, she couldn't give it up, not without trying, so she made application for the franchise and sent it to Austin with Hank Swain and hoped that somehow by spring she'd be able to get her hands on two coaches. Where, she had no idea, for Texas had been stripped of stages; every vehicle available was pressed into service with the Army fighting now on short rations and, if the latest rumor was true, short on ammunition.

The war, in spite of what people said and hoped, was drawing to a close. The Union troops were pushing the Southern army back on every front, and Yankee ships blockaded every port so that nothing went in or out.

It was a bad time, with bleak prospects for the future, and she wished that Dan Canby hadn't gone to California because she really didn't like being alone, making all the decisions and never sure that any of them were right.

Dan Canby was put ashore with his wagons in Acapulco, and the government officials were most cordial to him, and after a bit of wining and dining, he began to understand why. They felt that since so much merchandise was being transported through Mexico, a duty ought to be levied. Canby readily understood that this was going into their own pockets, and he remembered Buckley's advice about not fighting politics.

He offered them a proposition, outlining it carefully, about how he wanted to journey across Mexico and cross the Rio Grande at Piedras Negras. Of course, he would need a company of soldiers to guard the wagons.

Canby was assured that this was impossible, and a price was offered, which changed the melody of the song considerably, and after much wine and more talk he paid four hundred in gold and would pay another four hundred as the wagons crossed the river. In Mexican money this was a fortune, and the bargain was sealed.

They were talking about a distance of four hundred and seventy miles, across mountains and deserts, with the oxen making twelve miles a day in good terrain and five or six in bad. They were talking about sixty days of weather and heat and trouble, but when they crossed the river, there would be no Yankees waiting on the other side to take what had been so hard-earned.

Captain Christobal was in command of the soldiers, and Canby could not help but think about his position. He never fooled himself about how much any Mexican loved a Texan, and here he was, in the middle of some pretty lonely country with a hundred and thirty of them and sixty wagons loaded to the moaning axles.

The Mexican officials and Captain Christobal had already taken under-the-table money to make this journey possible, so Canby did not think for a moment that Christobal was above stealing the whole thing.

Alone, he was helpless and knew it and did not even bother to wear his pistols around the night camps. His weapon was words, and he spent his time talking.

"'There'll be five extra gold pieces for each of you when we reach Texas," he said to one group around the fire. This was a lot of money to them, and he knew it. "It is most important that we reach Texas, *amigos*. If we do not, there will be no money for you. Nothing for your families."

Canby would let this go around the camp; they were great talkers and discussed everything at length, important or not. And each night he would work on them. "When we get to Texas, each of you will have a job that pays well, in gold. It will feed your families and clothe your children. But we must reach Texas to do this."

They were all poor, and two pesos was a fortune; Canby was talking about dollar-a-day wages, and they listened carefully. "The goods on the wagons will bring much money in

Texas. And if I make the money, you will all have good jobs. We must guard the goods with our lives."

Day after day he kept this up, and he could not be sure whether or not he was making the impression he wanted to. The soldiers were doing some talking of their own, and Canby was sure they were trying to sway the drovers to their side.

"Each of you has a fine shotgun, a truly fine weapon," he pointed out. "With this weapon you can protect yourselves and the wagons so that when we get to Texas you will get your money and take it proudly to your wives."

Daily they moved eastward, relentlessly, paced by the plod of the oxen, which seemed to vary little, uphill or down. They crossed mountains and plains and rivers and endured the dust and the torrential rains, and the weeks stretched into a month, and he began to think that there would be no trouble from the soldiers.

Then a sergeant tried to break into one of the wagons, and a shotgun boomed, and the sergeant died there, and Christobal rushed to take charge of his troops. Canby, in his blankets when it happened, grabbed a long Green River knife and dashed toward the commotion.

Christobal had a squad lined up, and they covered the Mexican drovers, and Canby figured that the captain was making his move at last.

"What's going on here?" he said innocently and came up to Christobal, and before the captain could answer, Canby grabbed him around the throat and pressed the point of his knife against the flesh there. "Tell your men to put down their rifles, or I'll slit you from ear to ear!"

The captain started to struggle bravely, and Canby opened him up a little and made him bleed, and then Christobal gave the order. The Mexican drovers disarmed the soldiers, and the rifles and ammunition were distributed.

"We will have no more use for your services, captain," Canby said, shoving him away. "Take your horses and leave camp. Trouble us again and we'll leave you for the buzzards to pick clean."

The captain pressed a hand to the small gash on his throat. "It is a long way to Texas, *amigo*."

"We'll get there," Canby told him. "These men have families there, jobs there. Their children will go to school and learn to read there. You'd steal these wagons and the goods for a few gold pieces each because you don't know where your money is coming from tomorrow. Captain, these men earn money each week. They have work and honor, and they won't throw away tomorrow and all the other days to come for a few pieces of gold." He made a cutting motion with his hand. "Get out of this camp. Take your men and horses and get!"

"There are many *bandidos,*" Christobal said. "It is only the soldiers that keep them from attacking you."

"Why, I believe you're right there," Canby said. "Order your men to take their uniforms off. *Andale!*" He called to his wagon masters. "Sanchez! Cruz! Have your men dress in the uniforms."

In the firelight Christobal's complexion seemed to blanch. "Senor Canby, if we're without arms and dressed as peons, the *bandidos* will be on us before we travel a mile."

"Now you should have thought of that sooner," Canby told him. "When a man tries to be a thief, then he's got to take a few chances. Now strip!"

The first news that Amy Leland had that Dan Canby was in Texas was Hank Swain's hurried report the minute he got back from San Antonio. No, he hadn't seen Canby, but there was talk about the wagons and oxen that had crossed the river and were moving north. Likely they were on the San Antonio road right now.

This filled Amy Leland with a fluttery excitement, and she found that the days of waiting were incredibly slow. She hired a boy to watch the south road for them, and finally, weeks later, they were coming. The boy said they were only an hour away, but she didn't know about an oxen's slow, sure gait, so it was nearly two hours before they appeared at the end of the main street, coming on slowly, a sea of bowed, straining backs and rumbling wagons that left deep furrows in the soft earth.

Canby pulled up in front of his store and stopped, getting down carefully while a large crowd gathered. Amy Leland came out and looked up and down the street, and he watched her eyes as her gaze traveled from wagon to wagon.

Canby stepped up on the porch beside her, then signaled for one of the Mexicans to come over. He spoke fluent Spanish, and the Mexican nodded, went to one of the wagons, and broke open a case of canned peaches. He brought it to Canby, who took out the cans and tossed them into the air for the people there to catch.

"If you want more, you can buy at Canby's store," he said and laughed. Then he glanced at Amy Leland and saw that she was looking at the dismantled coaches in the last wagons. "I've got somethin' for you, Amy. A present from California."

"Are those mudwagons? Where did you get those mudwagons?"

"California. Nobody wanted 'em, so I took the wheels off and loaded 'em on." He frowned. "I thought—"

"Dan, I've been praying for coaches."

"You have? Ain't you been prayin' for me?"

"Field and Scully are building some coaches. I know they're after a mail contract."

"What contract?"

"I'll explain it later," she said, touching him on the arm. She looked up and down the line of wagons. "My, they're big, aren't they?"

"Big, heavy, and slow. But I'll tell you one thing. I brought them across Mexico through the damnedest terrain you ever saw, and not even an axle broke. Any way you look at it, they're plain hell for strong." He thumbed a match alight for his cigar.

"Where are the horses?"

"Sold 'em."

"You what!"

He grinned. "For eight times what they'd have brought in Texas." He took a thick money belt from beneath his shirt. "There's enough gold in there to really set us up in business."

"Say, I put up half of those horses, you know."

"Sure, and we're going to split right down the middle." He kept watching her and smiling. "Do you suppose I could get a bath and a shave? Then we could talk it all over after we've had supper."

"Well, I can't think of a better excuse. And I suppose there are a lot of details."

"Oh, yeah, hundreds at least." He rubbed the dirty front of his buckskin shirt and shifted powder horn and pistols and his long knife to the back of his hip. "When I met Hank Swain down the line, he told me you'd about sold me out. Once we get these wagons unloaded, I expect to wait on the counter while you ring the cash register. Just wait until you see these goods."

"Every time I look at your sign," she said, "I'm struck by the fact that it ought to read Canby & Leland. It would look much better."

He stepped down and backed into the street and looked at it. "Doggone if you ain't right." He grinned. "We'll talk about it over supper."

"I thought you said after."

"How about over?"

"All right. Now don't you think you ought to get to unloading before something is stolen?"

3

On April 9, 1865, General Lee met General Grant at Appomattox and the war was over, but the news of it did not reach Texas until May 22, and it was like the death of a loved one who has suffered a long illness—expected, yet hard to take.

To most Texans it meant that their sons and husbands and fathers would be coming home, not as they would have liked, victorious, but coming home just the same.

To the freighting company of Leland & Canby it meant that the newly signed mail contract was worthless; Texas, as a government, was bankrupt and would soon be under Yankee military law.

Amy Leland and Dan Canby talked it over thoroughly, and the firm of Canby & Leland threw all their cash resources into the stage line, and it nearly drained them. The erection of stage stations, the salaries, and the cost of the equipment maintenance used most of their capital. They were ready to begin passenger schedules and regular mail service, but they needed working money.

To back out now would be to lose it all, and to continue meant to go on paying the bills with no real income in sight. Texas, broke, beaten, politically confused, could not help them, and they didn't bother to ask.

The store was clear, and they really had no outstanding debts, no loans to repay; their problem was getting enough money so they could operate for a year. To try to borrow money from friends in the South was out of the question; everything was chaos, money worthless, prices gone sky-high, and nothing to buy. In New Orleans a pound of brown sugar sold for a dollar and twelve cents, and a pair of cheap Georgia duck pants went for eighteen dollars, gold.

Dan Canby decided to ride overland to San Francisco and find Ken Buckley and, if he could, establish a line of credit. The blockade was lifted, and ships regularly plied the gulf ports, and there was a railroad near completion across that strip of Panama; a man could expect a shipment to arrive in three or four months.

Once Canby had made up his mind, there was no stopping him; he found a rancher who agreed to sell him two good horses, and with one bearing his pack, he left town, not expecting to be back until late summer or fall.

Alone again, Amy Leland moved to the store and pondered her idle stagecoaches. It seemed a shame that they should sit there; they were magnificent vehicles, high and boxy, built to travel light over the roughest roads in any weather. They would carry eight passengers and three hundred pounds of mail.

Everything hinged on Canby's being able to borrow money. Still, it was better to gamble now, run the coaches while she could, and then if they went broke, it wouldn't be because they hadn't tried. So she had some signs made and sent Hank Swain out to distribute them.

LELAND & CANBY STAGES
ANNOUNCING
Northbound leaving Austin
each Wednesday noon for:
Fredericksburg
San Saba
Comanche
Abilene
Tascosa

Southbound leaving Tascosa
each Monday for southern
towns.

FARE:	$31.00, gold
MAIL:	25¢
FREIGHT:	6¢ lb.

She dispatched a coach north to Tascosa, and the driver had some notices to put up. Another went south to Austin to post notices and wait for departure time. Leland & Canby had no stage offices in either town, so they parked in front of the largest hotel and made up for their run there. The hotels didn't mind, because the passengers usually stayed there and took their meals there.

When the southbound came through Abilene, Amy Leland was there to meet it. Eight passengers crowded together inside, and four of the heartier breed rode the top. Hank Swain drove this run personally, and he waddled into her office, his jaws rapidly kneading his tobacco. Hostlers changed the mules while the passengers went down the street to eat and cut the dust out of their throats.

"Six hundred pounds of freight and two sacks of mail," Hank Swain said. He dug into his pocket for a leather poke and counted out a hundred and forty-four dollars in gold for the fares, over thirty dollars in mail money, and thirty-six dollars in freight. Then he grinned. "Once I posted them notices, folks almost fought to be on that stage, even for a short run. You want I should send another coach north before I pull out?"

"No, I'll take care of it."

"I can't wait to meet the northbound," Swain said. "How were the crossings?"

"Up pretty high on the banks, but the worst is over. No Injun trouble at all." He scrubbed his uncombed hair. "Sure is lonely country. Those stations seem mighty few and far between. Ought to be closer than thirty miles."

"That takes money, and we haven't got it," Amy said. She went with Swain and watched him leave town, then walked back to her office in the store, trying to still a rising sense of excitement. She knew better than to count on this kind of revenue; it would soon taper off and cut into the profits.

Doe Scully and Pete Field were standing on the walk, and she didn't see them until she started onto the porch, then she stopped. Scully said, "Feelin' kind of big, ain't you?" He nudged Pete Field and grinned. "As soon as we get our hands on some horses or mules, we'll give you some competition. Got three coaches built now and workin' on the fourth."

"You've got a blabbermouth," Field said heavily. "That mail contract don't mean a thing now. We can carry mail as well as you can. Passengers, too."

"You get your livestock and then tell me about it," Amy said and went on into the store. She watched Scully and Field through the window; they had their heads together, talking; then they went on down the street.

Competition was something she expected, and she was content to let it be Scully and Field, because they had a talent for being just a little late in everything they did. Now Dan Canby was something else; he was a man who recognized opportunity and seized it, and even before he'd come back from his first California trip, she had decided that it was better to join him than to butt heads with him.

During the month of May and well into June Amy Leland began to understand that somehow she was going to have to double her service; each coach that came through was filled to capacity and then some, with men riding on top and baggage lashed onto the sides and overflowing the boot. Amy tried to understand this migration, this desire to travel; conditions were uncomfortable at best, yet people who had no money managed to scrape together the fare, and often a few weeks later they would take a returning stage.

Soldiers were coming back in increasing numbers, and the mail volume picked up, almost doubling in thirty days, while the stage freight was limited only by the amount that could be carried.

Stage relay stations held Amy Leland back; she figured this was an even weaker link than not enough coaches. Thirty miles between stations kept the drivers from running the mules. If she could build stations between them, cutting the distance to fifteen miles, with a fresh change of mules, she could double the service and not have to buy any more coaches.

It was something to work on, and she kept her drivers on the lookout for mules, but they never found any.

The Yankee Army came in late June, two companies under the command of a stern-faced major, and they started to build a fort on the Elm Fork of the Brazos, about ten miles northeast of town. The Texans were sullen about this intrusion, but they showed no reluctance to work for the Yankees and never missed a pay day, for the money was gold, and that was always pretty hard to come by.

There was considerable gossip as to just what the Army intended to do in that part of Texas, and Amy Leland listened to the gossip and withheld her opinion; they'd know when the Army told them and not before. The major's name was Bolton, and he came into town with a long-legged sergeant, and they tied up in front of the store, and the sergeant went in ahead of the major as though he intended to sweep aside anything that might be in the way.

The clerk went into the back office and told Amy Leland they were in the store, and she came out, walking the length of the counter to where the major stood, rocking back and forth on his heels and stripping off his gauntlets.

"I'd like to speak to Mr. Leland," the major said. "I was advised that he could be found here." He was a strongly built man with a square, stern face and a voice capable of shouting orders over the clamor of battle.

"I'm Amy Leland. I'm a partner in this store and in the stage company."

The major frowned, a hairy gathering of his eyebrows. "Is your partner Mr. Canby?"

"Yes."

"I'll speak with him then."

"Mr. Canby is in California on business." She glanced at the sergeant, a man touching thirty; he had a semblance of a smile half-hidden beneath his fawn-colored mustache. "What is it you want, major?"

"I'm not accustomed to conducting business with a woman."

"And I'm not used to Yankee officers," Amy said. "So we're starting even, aren't we?"

For a moment it seemed that he would take offense; then he

smiled and took off his hat and laid it on the counter. "You're quite right there, Miss Leland. It is 'Miss,' isn't it?"

"Yes."

"I heard the name of Leland & Canby when my command halted one of your southbound stages," he said. "My name, by the way, is Harry Bolton." He offered his hand briefly, a strong, sincere grip. "I know you won't like this, but I'm going to be the military governor. The fact that you were operating mail and passenger service impressed me. I'd like to talk to you about it."

"Well, I have an office in the back room."

"That would be fine. Come along, sergeant." They went in back, and Amy saw that they had chairs and invited Bolton to light his cigar. "This is Sgt. Maj. Ben Talon. If we can reach any kind of agreement, you'll be seeing him from time to time."

"An agreement on what, major?"

"Perhaps I've gotten ahead of myself," Bolton admitted. "The military function here is varied. We are going to try to reestablish local, county, and statewide government on a graft-free basis." His smile was wry. "That may be optimistic, but we're going to do it. We also intend to work to improve the economic condition; Texas is broke, peddling worthless money and script. Under separate command, police forces are being recruited to maintain law and order, although that's not my province, thank God."

"What's the matter with them?" Amy asked.

"Why," Bolton said, "they're colored."

"That's insane! There'll be another war!"

"We hope not," Bolton said. "However, I think we'll have more than our hands full. We're supposed to put down any Indian trouble, in addition to the other duties I've mentioned. Miss Leland, we will need the help of as many citizens as we can enlist. An army lives on line of supply. And as it stands, we're pretty thin. Men are being mustered out by the thousands, and I consider myself fortunate to have two companies. Equipment is lying fallow in some of the frontier posts because we don't have the manpower to use it." He paused to flick ash off his cigar with his little finger. "I've seen your stage line, and it's a shoestring operation."

"Not because I want it to be. We just can't get mules or stages."

"I can get you three hundred mules," Bolton said, "and twenty stages. They're Army mudwagons and ambulances, but they can be converted." He leaned forward and spoke confidentially. "Texans will work for you when they won't for me. Sure, we're hiring them, but they're quitting, too, when they get two twenty-dollar gold pieces in their pocket. Loyalty is something we'll have to learn to live without, so I'm not going to waste my time asking you to do anything for me. I'm going to buy it right down the line. Interested?"

"I'm in business," Amy said. "Keep talking."

"Fort Phantom Hill is going to need supplies, transportation, mail service. We haven't the men, and I wouldn't spare them to that duty if I had them, so I'll make you this offer: freight at half rates, passengers at twenty percent off, mail and dispatches free. In exchange I'll put Sergeant Talon in charge of the detail to get you your mules and coaches. I'll give you twenty men. You provide forty. You can leave for Camp Beecher when you're ready."

"Where's that?"

"More than four hundred miles, as the crow flies, and through the Indian Nations to Kansas." He straightened in his chair. "I'll provide mounts. You provision them out of the store."

She considered it, feeling that she should hold her breath. Then she said, "Major, I'll be ready to leave by noon tomorrow. But why Leland & Canby?"

"Because you exist. We'll need you, and believe me, Miss Leland, you're going to need us." He got up and offered his hand again. "You'll provide wagons for the journey?"

"Yes. I'll meet you at your fort site at noon with my men."

He nodded and drew on his gloves. "Of course, when you say you'll be there, you really mean one of your representatives."

"No, major. I mean *I'll* be there."

"Remarkable," Bolton said. "We don't have that kind of woman back East."

"Oh, yes, you do. And they walked to Texas when they first came here," Amy said. She went out with them and went behind the counter and opened a glass cigar case. She took out a handful and laid them down. "Good Havana cigars from California, sergeant. I'd suggest they'd go best after evening mess."

Ben Talon glanced at Bolton, then picked up the cigars and put them in his pocket. "That's very thoughtful," he said and stepped back, again taking his place in the military system.

The major and the sergeant rode out of town, passing on down the street while everyone stood there and stared suspiciously, and Amy Leland watched them go, holding back the urge to dance on the porch in plain view of everyone.

She had many plans to make and set to them. There were two clerks in the store, and she could trust them to manage while she was gone. She sent a boy to the freight yard for Hank Swain. She told Hank of the offer and left him in charge. He would round up the men, the mules, and the wagons and bring them around back for loading after dark.

The store closed at nine, and it was a half hour later, while she was going over the books, that someone rattled the front door. She picked up a lamp and a sawed-off shotgun and went to see who it was. Raising the shade, she saw Sgt. Ben Talon standing there, grinning, with a huge fistful of wild flowers.

Amy opened the door, and Talon stepped inside, taking off his hat. Wheat-colored hair lay heavy over his ears. He handed her the flowers.

"For you," he said and then acted as though he didn't know what to do with his hands.

"Sergeant, did you ride to the post and then back to bring me these?"

"Yes, I did."

She smiled. "That was foolish. But very nice."

"Yep. But that was the way I felt about the cigars—foolish but nice." He stood there and looked at her, still smiling. "The major smokes cheap stogies, and you give me Havanas. That was foolish. But the thought behind it was nice."

"I didn't like the idea of one man smoking when another wanted to and couldn't," Amy said.

"All things can't be equal," Talon said. "There's always majors, and there's always sergeants. The two don't mix, not very good, anyway. How come you don't talk like the rest of these people? You got Yankee blood in you or something?" He held up his hand quickly. "Now don't get sore. I just can't get used to everyone talking so slow. Why, if they was to yell fire, the town would be burned down before they got it out."

"Sergeant, would you like some coffee and something to eat?"

"For a fact, I would."

"Just help yourself to whatever you want off the shelves. I'll stoke up a fire and make the coffee." She took the flowers and put them in a vase, then filled the coffeepot.

Talon came back, spearing peaches from a can with his knife. "Now I haven't had anything like this for a year," he said, leaning against the door. "Ain't you a little young to be in charge of so much?"

"Now what kind of a question is that?" She looked at him, studying him.

He shrugged. "Well, a man don't expect to find a pretty woman running a store and a freight line, that's all. It kind of staggered the major a little, although he didn't let it show. He's got a wife and daughters back in Indiana, and he's got some firm ideas on what a woman should do."

"And shouldn't?"

Ben Talon grinned. "Why, a man gets those first. Didn't you know?" He ate the last of the peaches, licked his knife, and then folded it and put it in his pocket.

Amy Leland watched him carefully. "Sergeant, sit down." He took a chair, and she leaned back against the wall and crossed her arms. "Illinois?"

"How did you know?"

"The way you talk. I went to school in St. Louis for five years." The coffeepot began to bump on the stove, and she pulled it back from the hot spot. "Aren't you a little young to be a sergeant major?"

"Yep." He tapped his head. "But I've got it here. Don't know what it is, but I've got it."

"I notice you limp and carry your left arm a little stiffly."

He let his eyes widen and smiled. "Now that's some looking, I'll say. Is there anything you miss?" He laughed softly.

"Minie ball in '62, and a sniper in '64. Just never did learn to zig when I should zag."

She let her expression change, and there was a sadness in her eyes. "The war seemed a long way from here, sergeant, then men came back, with an arm or a leg or an eye gone. It's hard to understand how it really happened, because you feel no pain, and they no longer remember it. All it means is waste. A terrible waste."

"Sure, that's all it is. To tell you the truth, I never thought I was fighting for anything. The rebels was out there, and they'd shoot first if they got the chance, so you tried to beat 'em to it. Now that never made much sense, because if both sides would have held their fire, the damned war would have been over before it started." He got up and felt of the coffee-pot, and she got two cups so he could pour. "I have two brothers. They didn't want to go to war any more than I did. Earl, the oldest, bought out for three hundred dollars; he got some poor devil on the other side of town to take his place. He was killed at the first Battle of Bull Run. Marvin, my other brother, didn't want to go, and Pa didn't have the money to buy him out, so I sold myself to someone else so Marvin could buy out." He shook his head sadly. "He died that fall of fever. Pa, too." He looked at her and found her gravely watching him. "That ain't something you'll get many Yankees to tell you about, how they bought out of going to war by paying someone else to take their place. But somehow I've lost my shame of it. It's all right with me if us Yankees didn't want to go to war and the Southern fellas all ran to sign up. There's enough room in this country for all them heroes."

"They didn't want to go, either," Amy said. "Not really. But the band plays, and politicians make speeches, and you go, and then you come back if you're lucky."

"Or maybe the lucky don't come back," Talon said. "You make good coffee. Is your man nice?"

"My man?"

"Sure, Mr. Canby."

"Now wait a minute, he's not my man!" She was on the edge of losing her temper and drew back. "Around town they'll tell you I've whipped a man raw for saying that out loud. You're new here, so I'll just tell you once."

"Didn't know you felt that strong about men," Ben Talon said.

"Not about men, but I'll choose when I'm ready."

"Well, I've got nothing against a woman taking her time. How about putting me on the considering list?"

"Women put *all* men on the list," Amy said. "Some are just eliminated quickly. Besides, you don't know me, Ben."

"I'll know you time we get back. You'll know me, too."

"What kind of country is it? Wild?"

He rolled his eyes. "Renegade border bandits and Injuns. We'll fight before we get back. Fight plenty. A man don't ride across; he shoots his way." He paused to drink some more of his coffee. "Everybody wants what the other guy's got. You take those mules and wagons, for instance. They're sitting there, and they'd rot there, and no one would buy 'em. But once we start back, the border gangs will gather, and they'll kill us for the wagons and mules. Lord knows what they'd do with 'em once they got 'em, but they'd kill us just the same."

"And the Indians?"

Ben Talon shrugged. "Who knows about 'em? You can't talk to 'em because you can't speak their language. I've known some scouts who claimed they could, but they were lying. A few words, maybe, but no more. The trouble is, Amy, we're just not nice to people, and as time goes by, we build up a flock of enemies that way. Indians are what we've made 'em, I guess. You just can't push a man around and expect him to appreciate it."

"Ben, the major said something about Negro police. Is that so?"

He nodded. "You've got some Yankees in Washington who think it's a downright shame you went and put us to the trouble of a war. I guess they've been thinking real hard, trying to figure out some way to make you pay for it."

"There's going to be a lot of trouble," Amy said softly. "And I don't want any part of it."

Talon finished his coffee and put the cup aside. "Trouble is something we all have plenty of. Mixing in it seems natural

enough. You might say that's our first talent, finding trouble."
He touched his fingers to the beak of his forager cap. "I'll be
looking for you around noon. You're not going to disappoint
me now and stay home, are you?"

"No," she said. "I won't disappoint you."

He turned and went out through the front of the store, and
after she heard his horse leave, she went and locked up, then
stood there in the darkness, remembering clearly how he'd
looked at her, and the prospect of forty days with this man
held shards of excitement for her.

"I'll have to keep you on the list," she said and went back
and got ready for bed.

4

KEN BUCKLEY enjoyed money. He didn't care to save it; rather he enjoyed the challenge of making it, and with the proceeds from the sale of his store, and other investments, he joined with two other men and formed a bank in San Francisco.

The war, the town, the location, the foreign trade, and the constant influx of people all blended to make it very malleable, and Buckley's partnership flourished at a surprising rate. Land prices rose steadily; a lot bought on Powell Street for a thousand dollars tripled in months, and everywhere new buildings were going up; there seemed to be no end to the money coming into the city.

Dan Canby had no difficulty establishing credit at the Bank of San Francisco; his friendship and reputation with Ken Buckley assured that. Canby was looking for three thousand dollars, but after two luncheons and an afternoon in Buckley's office, with his partners present, they rejected the loan of so small an amount. Texas was in for some difficult years, and the man who was solvent would end up on top, and they had no intention of backing a man who was destined to lose because he was shortsighted.

Buckley pointed out that Dan Canby was in trouble because he had always paid cash or borrowed no more than he needed, which left him eventually with the chore of getting more or losing what he had. They would, Buckley felt, extend him a line of credit, in gold, up to thirty thousand dollars, at ten percent, and as he needed more to keep up with a growing economy, they could extend the line to fifty thousand, sixty, and on up.

The Bank of San Francisco just did not want to back a loser.

With letters of credit in his pocket, Dan Canby sailed with four thousand dollars' worth of merchandise in the hold and had made arrangements to have another shipment follow within sixty days—firearms and ammunition and clothing and dried fruit and bulk flour and three tons of tinned stuffs. Behind him in San Francisco he was leaving Ken Buckley as his agent; a lot of arrangements had been made, and there was some hope in Canby's mind that shipments could be made overland, with his own wagons picking up the merchandise in Lawrence or Kansas City, and in that way reduce drastically the cost of the merchandise.

This time Dan did not enjoy the sea travel, but he endured it, and when he landed at Galveston, he found the Yankee Army in charge of everything. Two days were wasted in endless inspections, but he dispatched a rider to Austin with word that he wanted thirty wagons, and sixteen days later he was ready to load for the long drive north.

Impatient to get back, he took the stage from Austin and left the wagon train to follow, and when he arrived in Abilene and found that Amy Leland had been gone for nearly twenty-five days, he felt angry and depressed, and for several days the clerks steered a course around him until his normally good-humored disposition returned.

Camp Beecher was a wind-blown, nearly deserted post; the soldiers remaining spent their time on guard duty to keep looters from stealing everything that wasn't deeply planted. A weary captain was in charge, and he detailed men to provide all possible assistance to Sergeant Talon; the sooner he got rid of everything, the sooner he would be mustered out, which was his sole, consuming desire.

Amy Leland had her pick of the mules; she took ninety, and seven Army mudwagons, and all the spare parts she could find in the farrier's yard. The captain invited her to inspect the post and to take anything else she wanted, and she thought of the way stations she would have to build, so she took the stoves from three mess buildings and packed the coaches with pots and pans and boxes of knives and forks and tin dishes.

Over the evening cook fire, Amy Leland said, "I feel so guilty, taking all these things. Why, I must have two hundred blankets and good wooden bunks and furniture."

Ben Talon laughed softly. "After a war it's the junkman who gets rich." He shrugged and made an open-palm gesture. "What's the government going to do with all this stuff besides let it sit? There aren't enough men to fill the bunks, let alone take 'em apart and ship 'em back East to some warehouse. Hell, the war wasn't hardly over when some outfit in New York—ah—Bannerman—was in there buying up everything he could get his hands on. And I mean everything. Cannon, observation balloons—everything. So you take what you want, load as many wagons as you want. The captain will be pulling out one of these days with his company, and I'll lay you odds that within a week there won't be a stick standing." He paused to fill his tin cup from the coffeepot. "All the lumber you see will go into building new front porches or picket fences. You wouldn't want to be here when the captain leaves. People will fight like dogs for what they can pick up. Some good men are going to get killed. That's the way it goes."

"It doesn't seem right, Ben."

"Didn't say it was, but that's the way it'll be. Man isn't much, Amy. Just a dangerous animal that's been highly trained. Once in a while they forget the training and you've got war." He swished the coffee around to pick up the grounds in the cup, then splashed it into the fire, raising steam. "You asked me once how come I was a sergeant major at my age. Major Bolton was General Bolton four months ago. I was Captain Talon then. You see how things are? Same way here." He stood up and stretched. "We ought to leave in the morning. I'm taking four of the light artillery pieces with me."

"Why?"

"The border raiders let us pass through because we didn't have anything to steal. But goin' south it'll be different, and I figure the cannon loaded with grape will go a long way to discourage 'em." He grinned. "Besides, you can put one on each corner of the courthouse lawn when you get back, and they'll give a dinner in your honor for your civic pride."

"Sometimes I don't know when you're joking," she said.

They assembled at dawn, when the sky was barely turning light, and the wagons were all hitched with an eight-mule span although they would normally do with six; it was Ben Talon's way of handling the mules without having to herd them along.

A day took them thirty miles to the southwest, for the land was rolling and grassy and traveling was easy. They made close camp the first night with a heavy guard, and the next day they traveled with scouts out, and when one came back, it was as Ben Talon expected; the border bandits were flanking them each step of the way, keeping down just below the crown of the low, rounded hills.

"They're looking us over," he said to Amy Leland.

Six days took them to the Cimarron, six days of being watched and paced, and when they reached the crossing, Ben Talon knew they were going to have to fight. The border bandits needed the crossing; it would slow the wagons and mules down, pin them against the river so they could be cut to pieces and have no avenue of retreat.

"Get the cannon out of the wagons and mount 'em on the carriages." Talon passed this order back and at the same time ordered the drivers to start getting the mules and wagons across; it would take all of that day and perhaps a part of the next.

The approach to the crossing was a swale flanked by low hills, and the bandits appeared, mounted, at least a hundred and fifty of them, and they stood their high ground as though waiting for a signal.

Ben Talon didn't hesitate. "Fire some grape in there for effect," he said, and a fieldpiece boomed and reared on its trails, and suddenly a gap was rent among the mounted men.

"Fire! . . . Fire! . . . Fire!" Talon yelled, spacing his commands so that one artillery piece was always loaded. The grape shot tore into the hill, spouting geysers of earth but doing little damage because the bandits wheeled and passed out of sight and into safety.

The artillery was loaded and hooked onto the wagons and remained on the north bank, protecting the crossing, which went on through the night, following lanterns hung on rope strung from bank to bank.

Amy Leland was not sure what she thought of Ben Talon's opening fire on the bandits; a part of her mind told her that he was attacking first, a sound military move, and another part of her mind kept bringing her to the fact that the first burst had killed and maimed a dozen men.

Talon said nothing to her—no explanation, no apology; he acted as though it had never happened, although he never once relaxed his guard during the remainder of the trip.

They saw Indians and buffalo—many Indians but not so many buffalo—and Talon fired on the Indians to keep them back, but he had the cannon stuffed with powder and used dried mud balls for shot so that no real harm came to the Indians.

Amy Leland wasn't sure she understood that, either; Talon was a complex man, with rigid personal codes which he lived by. There was no mercy in him, yet he was merciful.

He'll take some figuring out, Amy thought to herself.

Forty-seven days after she left Abilene, Amy Leland returned. She had so many mules that a temporary corral had to be built to hold them, and the mudwagons crowded the freight yard. Nearly everyone in town came to see them, and she looked around for Dan Canby, expecting to find him, for she was sure he had returned by now.

But she didn't see him.

Major Bolton and a squad were in town; he rode up and dismounted and stood with his hands on his hips, looking at the crowded yard. Sergeant Talon rode up and swung off, and the major said, "What the devil did you bring the cannon for?"

"Going to put them in the courthouse yard, sir."

"You're joking, sergeant."

"No, sir, I think they'll look real nice there." He grinned at Amy Leland. "I've brought you this far, so I guess it's all right for me to walk you to the store."

"I've been waiting for the offer," she said. "There's a few things I want to tell Hank Swain—"

"Go ahead," Talon invited. "I'll chew the fat with the major."

Bolton brought out a cigar, then offered one to Talon. "I was beginning to worry about you, Ben. You took a long time."

"Well, we didn't push very hard. Get the post finished?"

"Just about. Some roofing to be done on one or two sheds." He frowned. "The police unit moved in on us—three squads. White officer, but the troopers are colored. None of us like it, but what can we do?" He puffed nervously on his cigar. "I feel sorry for the troopers; they don't want to be here. They're not trained, and they don't want trouble. You haven't met Canby yet, have you?"

"No, sir."

"I'll be interested in your opinion, Ben. Will you be coming back to the post tonight?"

"Yes, sir, I probably will."

"Stop at my quarters then," Bolton said and mounted his horse.

Amy Leland came out with Swain; she introduced him, and Swain grinned and wiped his hand on his pants before offering it.

"Nice to meet you there, saajint. Heard your name mentioned here and there." He turned his head and looked at the crowded yard. "We sure are set up in business now. Sure are."

"How's your ox freight coming along?"

"Hate 'em," Swain said. "But the Mexicans can handle 'em just fine. It takes some doin'. Man, they get to fightin' and gorin' one another, and I'd as soon be in another county. But the Mexicans do all right. Must have forty or more workin' the freight wagons now." He turned and looked again at the mules. "Some of them is for the freight wagons, ain't they?"

"Stages," Amy said. She glanced at Ben Talon. "I'm ready."

"And I've been waiting. It's been some years since I've walked a pretty woman up the street." He offered his arm, and she took it; they moved along the walk, and the sun beat down, bounced from the dusty street, and reflected harshly off the walls of the buildings.

Halfway down, a painter was working on a sign: Abilene Citizens' Bank. D. Can—

Amy stopped and looked at the sign, then said, "Well, what do you know!"

They mounted the porch of the store and stepped inside; Dan Canby was behind the counter, reading a newspaper, and he didn't put it down until Amy stepped up and rattled a tin canister. "Hey," she said, "what are you sore about?"

"When I leave a partner in charge of something," he said, "then I expect her to be here when I come back."

"I couldn't pass this up, Dan. You ought to understand that."

"Well, I don't care to talk about business in front of strangers."

"Ben's not a stranger," Amy said.

"He is to me," Canby snapped. "But I guess you two got to know each other right well."

Ben Talon took off his cap and mopped his face with his neckerchief. "Tell you what, Canby, it's a hot day, and we're all worn to a frazzle, and likely we're ready to lose our tempers at everyone. So why don't I just say good day and—"

"You can make it good-bye as far as I'm concerned!"

"Dan, that's no way to be," Amy snapped.

"It's the way I am—take it or leave it."

She held her temper. "Dan, I don't think we ought to be giving each other choices to make. Now why don't you crank up the cistern and get us all something cold to drink?" She waited, but he made no move away from the counter. "Why didn't you come to the freight yard and meet me, Dan? What were you doing? Standing here, sulking?"

"Don't talk to me like that," he said quickly.

"Why don't we all change the subject?" Talon invited pleasantly. "I think we'll get rain this summer."

"When I want your bell to ring," Canby said, "I'll pull your rope."

"That sounds fair enough," Talon said, replacing his cap. He smiled and looked around the store. "I've got a hankering for some more of those peaches. Like to take a couple of cans back to the post with me."

"I've never sold you any pea—" Canby closed his mouth as Amy Leland went around the counter, got two cans, and set them in front of Ben Talon. Canby put out his hand and kept Talon from picking them up. "Twenty cents apiece."

"Take it out of my share," Amy said.

"I want him to pay for 'em."

"And I want him to have them. What's it going to be, Dan? Make up your mind in a hurry now because you won't get a chance to change it later."

He looked at her, saw that set of the jaw and the unwavering eyes, then laughed and pushed the cans toward Ben Talon. Then he smiled, and the irritation drained away from him, and he said, "Talon, you've just seen Dan Canby give his impersonation of a jackass."

"My ears were beginning to feel a little long myself," Talon admitted. "To be real honest with you, I knew I wasn't going to like you the minute I looked at her. But I've learned that she isn't mine, and she isn't yours."

"You learn quicker than I do," Canby said. "And I'll have to remember that. How about some chilled cider?" He went on in back, leading the way, and cranked up the cistern.

They talked and drank nearly a gallon of cider. "—Buckley's really struck it rich in California," Canby was saying. "Lord knows how much money he made in the store business, but if I know him, he salted most of it. Anyway, he's in the banking business with two other men, and he established a line of credit for me."

"Is that why you're opening a bank down the street?" Amy asked.

"Sure. Makes sense, doesn't it? With thirty thousand dollars in credit, I'd be a fool not to make it work for me. Look at it this way: I've got thirty thousand put aside in Buckley's bank for me to use, as much as I want, when I want; I just draw against the account and pay ten percent interest on what I use. All right, that means that here in Texas I'm sitting on one big pile of Yankee dollars. So with just a few thousand in cash, which will cost me ten percent, and the credit to back me, I'm in the banking business, making loans, accepting deposits, which in turn I'll loan on the right security so that in the long run I can use Buckley's money for nothing, profit here canceling out the interest. And unless things go really bust, I may get enough ahead until I have my own finances, my own credit."

"Well, now, partner," Amy said, "how about financing the building of ten way stations so I can expand my service?" She glanced at Ben Talon and winked. "Because you're such a sorehead, you didn't see the mudwagons and eighty mules I got off the Army. All the way back I've been figuring out how best to use the mules and coaches, and I think I'd be a fool not to expand."

"To where?" Talon asked.

"Well, there's Cameron and Waco and Dallas and on up through Paris to Fort Smith, Arkansas." She looked from one to the other. "What's wrong with that? Scare you a little?"

"That's a lot of territory," Ben Talon said gravely. "It's being spread mighty thin."

"I think we ought to move before anyone else does," Dan Canby said. "You're shortsighted, Talon. There's a tide to everything."

"It's a gamble I wouldn't take," Talon said. "Personal opinion."

"But it's one I'll take," Dan Canby said. "By golly, yes. We'll get started on it right away, just as soon as we get the line from Austin running on increased schedule."

"And I've been thinking about that, too," Amy admitted. "Scully and Field have four coaches. Why couldn't we make a deal with them? Let them run as independents and use our stations. We'll charge for it. It's either that or nothing at all for them. They're too late for anything else."

"I don't know about hooking up with those two," Canby said.

Talon, with his chair tipped back and cold cider in his glass, said, "Did I hear you right? Did you disagree with her about something?"

"He knows I'm right," Amy said. "Scully and Field can be pests. My way they'll be too busy to be a bother. And we can use the added service and collect a station stop fee. I'll even rent them the mules to get started."

"Good point there," Canby said. He heard the bell jangle over his front door and got up and went out.

They could hear him talking, and there was the soft melody run of a woman's voice, and Amy Leland started to get up, but Ben Talon put out his hand and pushed her back.

"Don't do that, Ben. I want to see."

"You get to see too much as it is," he said. "Drink some more cider."

"You can be pretty bossy at times. I don't know whether I like it or not."

"Something a woman has to get used to. A man, too. Each one needs a little telling off now and then."

"And you know just when that time is?"

"Yep. Figure I've got that much sense."

She studied him at length over the rim of her glass. "You don't approve of me doing all this, do you?"

"I see no harm in it. But there'll come a day when you'll give it up."

"Ben, I just can't see that day."

"It'll come. You're a woman, and what a woman needs she can't get out of ledgers or a fat bank account."

"My, that's pretty smug, Ben."

"Well, it's the truth. Coat it any way you like."

He looked around as a woman spoke from the doorway. "I thought I heard voices back here." She was in her mid-twenties, very fair, and quite tall. Her face was squarish, but she had good eyes and lips that smiled nicely. She looked at Amy Leland, saying, "When Daddy drove me into town and I saw all those mules, I just knew you were back, Amy. You look so nice tanned."

"Ben, this is Emily Vale. Sgt. Ben Talon."

He got up, and Emily gave him her hand. "I heard about you, sergeant. You must pay us a visit at the ranch. It's eleven miles due south. You can't miss it."

"If my duties permit," he said.

"Surely they must give you time off, sergeant." She turned when Canby came up. "If you'll have the clerk set everything out back, we'll pick it up before leaving town."

"Would you like some cold cider?" Canby asked.

"Is it hard?"

"No, but it's got a tang." He poured a cup and handed it to her. She drank some and wrinkled her nose and smiled. "I had some hard cider once, when I was twelve. Grandfather used to make it, and I found where he hid it. Everyone was properly disgraced." She finished the cup and handed it back.

Ben Talon blew out his breath and put on his cap. "Like it or not, I've got to get back to the post. It's been a pleasure, Miss Vale."

"My daddy says you Yankees are going to rub our noses in the dirt. Is that so, sergeant?"

"No, that's not so," Talon said.

"Daddy won't believe that."

"If I see your daddy, I'll tell him that," Ben Talon said. "And if he's got a lick of sense, he'll believe it. I'm as sick of the war as you are. Do you believe that?"

"I lost kin. Two brothers. Another came back with one arm. Who pays for that, sergeant?"

"Nobody. How could they?" He watched her carefully, then asked, "Why do you want me to come out to your ranch?"

"So my daddy and all the men there can beat your Yankee head off," she snapped. He continued to study her, no expression on his face, then she started to wheel away, but he caught her by the arm and held her.

"You've had your say," Talon said softly. "Now you stand pat and hear what I've got to say. Didn't your daddy get his craw full of fighting? Wasn't losing two of his boys enough? Or is it just a girl talking? A girl who's hurt and wants to hit out and don't quite know who to hit?"

"I—let me go!" She started to cry.

"So you can run? Where are you going to run to? Where can any of us go now? We killed each other, and now we've got to live together. Maybe we can't, but we have to try." He let go of her arm. "I'll be out to see you one of these days. Maybe you'll play the spinet for me, and we'll sit in the shade and talk, and maybe out of it all will be something to take the place of what we have now."

She dried her eyes with the back of her hand and watched him. "I—have to go." She started to turn, and then looked back at him. "It hurts to lose. It really hurts."

"I know."

She left the store, and Dan Canby gnawed on a cold cigar, his expression grave. Then he said, "Talon, you've fooled me. I'll have to watch you."

"If you want to waste your time," Ben Talon said, then went out and walked down the street to his horse.

5

LELAND & CANBY began stage service to Fort Smith, Arkansas, in September, when the steady rains began and the buffalo started to move south and the Indians were too busy hunting to bother the stages.

One of the first southbound passengers was a tall man with dark hair and a clipped mustache and carrying a silver-headed cane. He endured the tedious days of jolting and suffered the indifferent meals in the stage way stations, and in time—although he thought that time would never come—he arrived in Abilene.

Without delay he ordered a room at the hotel and instructed the clerk to have tub and water brought up for his bath, a thing that gave him away immediately as a dude. An hour later, dressed in a fresh suit, he left the hotel and walked toward the adobe office of Leland & Canby, knocking with his cane on the heavy door.

A clerk let him in. "I would like to see Miss Leland," he said crisply.

There was another clerk; he looked up, then a door farther down opened, and Amy Leland said, "Sam, I want you to go over these freight manif—" She saw the man standing there, and she smiled and hurried to him. "Taylor. Taylor Blaine. Why, what on earth are you doing in Texas?" She took his arm and led him into her office and closed the door.

He looked around, at the rich furniture and tapestries and ornate lamps. "Very plush," he said, removing his hat and gloves. "Very."

"Oh, this." She laughed and sat down, smoothing her

skirt. "My partner brought them from California, for my house. But I never got around to building one." She nodded to another door leading back. "When I had the office built, I had the room added. That's where I live. This is a combination living room and parlor." She bent forward, her hands clasped together, her expression warm. "Taylor, it's so good to see you."

"Why, I believe you mean that."

"Of course I do. Why shouldn't I? Did you come here on business?"

"In a way. Business, yes, but I could have sent someone." He had a gaunt face, darkened a bit from the sun, and strong eyes that looked at everything directly. "A month and a half ago I had occasion to ship some cutting equipment to Paris, Texas. I routed it on one of your freight wagons, Amy, and it struck me that much too much time had passed since your last letter, and since there are certain opportunities here that I want to investigate, I decided to come myself." He spread his hands and smiled. "Really very simple."

"But very nice," she said. "Will you be staying here in Abilene?"

"A good part of the time," Blaine said. "I want to open an office here and another in Tascosa, if suitable personnel can be found."

"What kind of office?"

"Hide buying. Buffalo and cowhide."

She pursed her lips. "Most of the buffalo hunters sell their hides at Fort Larned. I don't run wagons there, Taylor."

"Yes, I know. I was thinking of shipping to Fort Smith. If my hide buying is successful, I'd like to talk about a contract."

"You mentioned cowhide. Are you in the cattle buying business?"

"Hide buying," he said. "There's a tremendous market for beef in the North, but unfortunately I have no way of shipping it there. Hides are an entirely different matter. I don't suppose I'll have any trouble renting office space?"

"No. Several business places have gone broke. They'd be glad to rent."

He got up and took her hand. "Amy, I'm staying at the hotel. Will you have dinner with me?"

"Tonight?"

"Yes. About seven?"

"That would be fine," she said and walked to the front door with him. He bent and kissed her hand and then walked on, passing Dan Canby, who was walking toward the freight office.

"Now who the devil was that dude?" Canby asked Amy.

"A gentleman I knew in St. Louis."

"Yeah, just how well?"

"We were once engaged," she said.

He turned and had a final look before Blaine turned into the hotel. "Taylor Blaine?"

"In person. Come on inside; I don't want you to display your temper on the street." She went back into the office and closed the door; he sat down and lit a cigar. "Taylor's family is pretty big in the leather goods business. He wants to set up an office and buy hides and ship them to Fort Smith."

"He's too far south for buffalo," Canby said.

"Cowhide, too, Dan."

Canby laughed. "The country may be way overstocked with cattle, but these ranchers won't sell hides and leave the beef to rot. What would he offer a head? A dollar?"

"Twenty-five cents," Taylor Blaine said evenly and became the first carpetbagger these people had ever seen. They were in his office—George Vale with his enormous frown, and Owen Kirby with nearly fifteen thousand head of beef that he couldn't give away, and Fred Early who owned nearly a whole county to the south.

Dan Canby was there, and several other people who had a passing interest in Blaine & Co., St. Louis.

Owen Kirby spoke for all of them. "If you meant that as a joke, sir, I'll laugh, even though it's a bad one. But if it was not a joke—"

"I never joke about business," Blaine said. "My offer, gentlemen, is twenty-five cents a hide, delivered to the freight yard for baling and shipment."

George Vale said, "Even if I would, I couldn't afford to

have my steers slaughtered for that price. And I'm not about to leave meat to rot on the prairie."

"Very well," Blaine said evenly. "But I pay cash, in gold, in case any of you want to change your mind. I would like to ship four thousand hides by the end of this month."

"None of mine," Fred Early said and left, stamping his boots angrily. Blaine looked at the others; they shook their heads and walked out.

Dan Canby remained, gently puffing his cigar and rolling it between his lips. "A quarter is damned little, Mr. Blaine. I'm surprised that you'd offer it."

"Oh, I'd have gone up," Blaine said. "But unfortunately they didn't care to discuss it." He tipped back his chair. "I haven't thanked you properly for getting me this office and finding the men to repaint it."

"Since you bought the paint from my store and I kept ten percent of the rent, I figure there is no need to thank me."

Taylor Blaine laughed. "I can appreciate a man who is ready to grab every dime that comes his way. There are a lot of opportunities. Be a shame to miss any of them." He took a bottle from his desk drawer, and two shot glasses; filling them, he handed one to Dan Canby. "In the two weeks I've been here, I've learned a good deal about your—situation. These cattlemen are against the wall, Canby. The market is simply too far away."

"Seems like it, but I hear that a fella named Goodnight is talking about driving north."

"I expect he's going to stop off at the moon while he's at it," Blaine said, and they both laughed. "Why, if they could make it, it would take eight months to get there and get back." He shook his head. "I'm afraid they're going to have to wait for the railroads, and that, my friend, is a long way away." He paused to light a cigar. "I hear that the Negro police are having a devil of a time with these Texans."

Canby nodded. "During the war there were some outlaw bands stealing in the name of the Confederacy. By the time the war ended, some of them were wanted by so many sheriffs that they couldn't come home. Now, since one man is just about as poor as another, they've got nothing to steal. So they fight the police. Not much trouble around here, but I hear that up near the border there's been several police killed."

"It's too bad these men don't have gainful employment," Blaine said. "How many of these—outlaws do you think there are?"

Dan Canby thought a moment, then said, "There was close to fifty or sixty in one gang that used to come into town."

"I don't suppose you ever see any of these men any more."

"Now and then I do. They try not to draw attention to themselves." He studied the end of his cigar a moment. "Mr. Blaine, you're talking like a man with business on his mind. Why don't you just come out with it? I'm not a man who's surprised easily."

Taylor Blaine laughed. "I should have known you were a liberal-minded man. Naturally, in the leather business, I can't help but think of a cow as anything more than hide. I suppose, because there's no place to sell the beef, that these —ah—independent businessmen never bother with stealing them."

"What's the use?"

"Exactly. But I am interested in buying hides."

"Just how much is a hide really worth?" Canby asked.

"At the railhead in St. Louis about four dollars and fifty cents. Tanned, about ten dollars. On the prairie, right here, about a dollar seventy-five."

"More like two dollars and seventy-five cents," Canby said. "Don't try to fool me, Blaine. I like straight talk, straight dealing."

Taylor Blaine shrugged. "Very well. My company would pay two seventy-five right here in Abilene." He drew deeply on his cigar and partially screened his face with smoke. "The range is crowded with unbranded cattle. How many would you say, Mr. Canby? Ten thousand head?"

"Twice that, if you wanted to be fussy and take only the unbranded ones. That's what you're trying to say, isn't it? That we ought to start a little business?"

"It was a thought. Interested?"

"How much profit is in it?"

"A dollar for you and a dollar for me and seventy-five cents for the gentlemen who kill and skin. Providing, of course, that you can make the arrangements with the—independent businessmen."

"I can do that," Canby said. "But it'll take organization. The hides will have to be brought here and—"

"I'll take complete charge of that," Blaine said. "When can we get started?"

"This weekend. One is bound to come in for supplies. I'll talk to him then." He took a final drag on his cigar and dropped it into the spittoon. "Blaine, I'd like to suggest that you be very careful and take only unbranded hides. It's going to be risky as it is, and there'll be some trouble."

"Why, to be expected. Any time a man sets out to make twenty thousand dollars, there's going to be trouble over it. Amy Leland will freight the hides, won't she?"

"Why ask me?"

"Because you're her partner."

"Hell, you were engaged to her!"

"Some time ago," Blaine said. "I would rather rely on your influence than mine."

"All right, I'll guarantee that she'll haul the hides."

"Then I rather think we have a business deal," Blaine said. "Shake on it?"

"Sure. I'm sure you can count accurately."

"But of course. This is a legitimate business, Canby. Everything aboveboard. We are in the business of buying hides, and each one is inspected, and since there are no brands or other marks of ownership, we must assume that the hide is the property of the seller. Right?"

"Right as rain," Canby admitted, getting up. "I'll be in touch."

That evening Taylor Blaine tried very hard not to complain about the bill of fare at the hotel, but the beef was Texas beef, tough as a cinch strap, and the potatoes tasted of dirt, and the greens lacked a certain leafy tastiness to which he was accustomed. The pie, his remaining hope, was a dismal affair —canned peaches wedged between a burned crust and a soggy one.

He gave up and settled for coffee stout enough to float an

eight-penny nail. Cream cut it a little, and sugar killed the gall of it, which made it fit for him to drink.

"You certainly don't have much of an appetite," Amy Leland observed.

"I'm just not hungry." He sighed and leaned back in the chair. "I suppose you heard that I had no luck at all with the cattlemen."

"Twenty-five cents a hide—why, you insulted them, Taylor! What did you really expect?"

"Well, to bargain at least."

She shook her head. "You're not in St. Louis now, Taylor. Men bargain only when they can afford it. These men are on their heels, and they're mighty run over. They've lost their taste for haggling. They took your price as a final offer. I thought you understood that."

"Well, I'm sorry. I didn't. I could go to a dollar."

"If you want, I can see that word gets passed around."

"Certainly appreciate it," he said. "After all, if I can't buy hides, then my venture is a failure." Then he laughed. "But surely they'll sell. In time they'll have to. Money is money, Amy." He reached out and patted her hand. "I would say, on the surface of things, that you're in a very good business, and I'll be surprised if you don't make a lot of money."

"I don't think it's just the money," she said.

"It would be with me, and I'm not ashamed to admit it. Surely you don't intend to stay here, Amy."

"Why not?"

"Well, you weren't overjoyed at the prospect of coming back."

"I know, but I'll stay now."

"There certainly are a lot of opportunities here, if a man had some investment capital. After all, these big ranchers can't expect to hold onto all their land. They'll have to let some of it go, and there are farmers who would pay ten dollars an acre for it if a man held out for it."

"Taylor, let me give you some good advice. Don't talk about farmers here, or joke about them, or refer to them, or suggest that you even know what a farm is."

He reared his head, surprised. "Why, for heaven's sake?"

"Because it sets the Indians off on a rampage. They see a

plow and know that some mucklehead is going to turn the grass over and kill off the buffalo. And it makes a cattleman see red because a farmer doesn't have much land, and to protect it, he builds a fence."

He nodded. "Advice well taken. I'll stick to hide buying."

Doe Scully and Pete Field owned four wagons, and Canby persuaded Amy Leland to sell them the oxen because they were going into the hide-hauling business. She thought that was ridiculous, because Taylor Blaine hadn't contracted for any hides, but to get the two men out of her way, she went along with Dan Canby.

They left town and weren't seen for nearly a month, mid-October, but when they returned, they had ninety bales of hides, ten to a bale. This caused a stir in town, and Blaine put them into his warehouse, then made arrangements to ship them north immediately.

Sgt. Maj. Ben Talon returned to town, one arm in a sling; he had been doing battle with some renegade Kiowas over on the Brazos, but that was done now, and he was given twenty days' leave while his wound healed.

The wagons were in Amy Leland's freight yard, making up for the trip north, when Talon swung down, looked them over, then went inside. The weather was nippy and the sky gray overcast, and a chill wind was whipping up dust on the street. He knocked at Amy Leland's office and then went in. She had the stove going, and he took off his coat, carefully moving it around his bad arm.

"Ben Talon, what happened to you?"

"The Kiowas are learning to shoot some better," he said, smiling. "Is that coffee there or Hank Swain's mud?"

"Coffee, made by myself. I'll get a cup."

When she handed it to him, he said, "I've missed you, Amy. When those Kiowas were trying to do me in, I thought of you, and it kept me going."

"Oh, you're lying." She moved a chair around for him. "I suppose you're going to be in and out again?"

"Nope. Got twenty days this time. Seems kind of fortunate, too." He scratched his mustache. "I couldn't help noticing those hides you're getting ready to ship. They represent a lot of steers rotting on the prairie."

"Yes, but it's not my responsibility, Ben. I contracted to haul them, that's all."

"They also represent some pretty mad Texans," Talon mentioned. "Kirby and Vale and Early went to see the major about it. Someone's cleaning the range of unbranded stock, butchering it for the hides, and leaving the carcasses. They want the Army to step in."

"Is the major going to do that?"

Talon shrugged. "Don't see how he can. The stock is unbranded. Hell of it is, the cattlemen could round it up, brand it, and claim it for themselves if they had the money to pay the wages of a roundup. Vale and the others didn't like being turned away. Can't blame them. They have no market, but it goes against everything they believe to see beef killed for hides."

"There are a lot of things going on, Ben, that we don't like. Dan opened a bank."

"Heard about it. Very enterprising fella, Dan is. He'll either end up owning it all or get in a hole so deep he can't see the sky. A man's very likely to pull something out of joint reaching so far." He got up and refilled the coffee cup. "You do make good coffee. How are you at fixing breakfast?"

"Why do you want to know?"

He smiled. "Someday I might ask you to marry me, and I wouldn't want to get up first morning and find you couldn't fry an egg." He came over and sat on the edge of her desk and studied her intently. "Amy, you go on being a big business tycoon. I'll wait."

"What will you wait for, Ben?"

"That day when you'd rather be a woman." He put the cup aside and gingerly got into his coat. "I'm going out to the Vale place."

"You don't see anything in her," Amy said.

"Now, I never said I did." He smiled again and went out and got into the saddle and rode out of town.

By his figuring, he should make the house around dark, and he felt sure he could spend the night in the bunkhouse and come back the next morning. He rode easily across miles of open, wind-brushed prairie, staying when he could to the crests of the low rolling hills.

He was three hours southwest of town when he saw twenty or thirty men—he couldn't be exact at that distance—rounding up cattle, hitting them on the head with sledgehammers while Mexican skinners got the hides. There were two wagons being loaded, and as he rode on, in a direction that would have passed him near them, one man mounted up and came to meet him.

Ben Talon stopped and sat his horse while the man came up, a dirty-faced man in bloody buckskin pants and cotton shirt. He carried a rifle across the saddle and kept his finger in the trigger guard as he stopped.

"What you snoopin' around for?" the man asked.

"Is that what I was doing?"

"I asked you a question, mister." He looked at Talon's chevrons and smiled. "I know you. You're the Yankee major's dog robber."

"And I'll bet everyone knows you because you've got the biggest mouth in Texas," Talon said frankly. "You want something? Tell me about it then, and I'll be on my way."

"You alone out here?"

"No, there's a whole company behind me. You can't see 'em because they painted themselves the color of the grass."

"Mister, it's been some time since I've killed a Yankee, but I ain't forgot how."

"That so?" Talon asked. "What's your name? I ask because I want to see that it gets put on your grave marker if you so much as curl a finger around that trigger."

The man stiffened and stared, then said, "You ain't seen anything out here." He wheeled his horse and rode back, and when he was out of rifle shot, Talon went on.

He rode for another two and a half hours, then saw the ranch buildings off slightly to the right and cut that way. When he rode into the yard, a dozen men appeared, all carrying firearms.

They circled him as he dismounted, and he looked at each of them and said, "Ain't you heard? The police have passed a law against you owning guns."

One spat tobacco and said, "This ain't mine. I took the loan of it from him." He nodded to another man.

And he said, "I borrowed this from a friend."

"I'll bet you all did," Talon said and stepped onto the porch.

George Vale came out with his fierce mane of hair and his scowl. "I offered no Yankee an invite to this place," he said.

"Your daughter did."

The old man turned his head and bellowed and a moment later Emily came out. She put her hands to her mouth when she saw who it was, and George Vale took her by the arm. "Did you invite him here?"

"Yes, Papa."

He sighed and nodded. "Come in then. I still remember my manners." His glance touched Emily. "This is somethin' I mean to discuss with you."

"She didn't mean the invitation," Ben Talon said, and the old man looked around. "I'm imposing, that's for sure, but you'd be interested to know that there's some skinning going on about eight miles north of here. About thirty men and two wagons."

George Vale swore and clenched his teeth until knots of muscle stood out along his jaw. "Someday I'm going to have to take my gun and kill a few men," he said. "Come in, sergeant. Supper's on soon." He opened the door and held it open. "My son Jonas is out, but he'll be back. He's a bitter man, sergeant. I'd thank you to let me handle any matter that comes up."

He went on down the hall, and Emily spoke in a whisper. "Oh, why did you come here?"

"To see you," Talon said. "Isn't that a good reason?"

"But I don't want to see you."

"Are you sure?"

"Yes, I'm su—oh, I don't know. I've got to see to supper." She turned and ran down the hall. Ben Talon watched her go, then he went on down and stepped into the parlor, where George Vale was taxing his hospitality and pouring a drink for his Yankee guest.

6

THE TABLE had been set for seven: George Vale, his housekeeper—a small-boned woman with gray hair and a shy smile—and Emily and her two younger sisters and brother Jonas, who had not yet returned to the house.

And Sgt. Ben Talon, who did not seem ill at ease at all, not even when George Vale asked him to say grace.

The meal was simple in the extreme—meat, potatoes, and cabbage—but Vale made no apology for it. There was very little talk; the women remained silent because it was their place, and Vale had nothing to say.

Finally Ben Talon said, "I've been over on the Brazos. The carpetbaggers are really moving in around Palestine."

George Vale raised his head quickly and looked at him. "What did you say?"

"I said I'd been over on the—"

"You used a word, sir—"

"Carpetbagger?" Talon laughed. "That's what you people call 'em, isn't it? I don't know a name that fits better. They're buying up land. No one wants to sell, but a lot of people are in the fix you're in—lots of land and cattle but no cash—so rather than lose it all, they sell some and hope to keep going on the cash." He shook his head. "It just doesn't work, Mr. Vale. There's still no market, and then you have farmer troubles on top of it."

"You don't like farmers, sergeant?"

"Sure, they're all right, but this isn't farming country. Not enough water. A man who was blind in one eye and couldn't see out of the other could tell that." He sighed and pushed back his empty plate. "Well, the carpetbaggers are like an army of ants; they'll be coming this way soon. If everyone holds out, they'll leave. It's the quick profit they're after."

"Like Taylor Blaine?" Vale asked. He leaned his elbows on the table and looked steadily at Talon. "Let me ask you a blunt question, sergeant. Is it true that a Yankee who didn't want to fight could pay someone else to take his place in the draft?"

"Yes. Two of my brothers did it."

Vale seemed stunned into a moment of silence. "You can admit this?"

Talon laughed softly. "Sir, how can I deny it when it's the truth?"

"It's a thing I would never admit," George Vale said softly. "I just don't think I could bring myself to it. I'd feel something. Shame, anger, something."

"I feel something," Ben Talon said. "But I don't pretend my way through life, Mr. Vale. I don't think I like people who do."

There was a stamping of boots in the hall, and a man's rough voice, then Jonas Vale stepped to the archway of the dining room and stopped there. He was twenty-one or -two, and his face was still boyishly smooth. His clothes were dusty from long riding, and he carried a pair of heavy pistols, although one sleeve was pinned back at the elbow.

He strode into the room and stopped by Ben Talon's chair. "I saw his horse, and I couldn't believe it." His voice was tight with anger, and he looked at the women. "Please leave the room."

"There'll be no trouble here," George Vale said. "Sit down, boy. Your supper's cold."

Jonas Vale put his hand on Ben Talon's shoulder, fisting a bit of his shirt. "I took an oath to kill any Yankee who stepped into this house," he said.

Without exerting himself, Talon knocked Jonas Vale's hand away and watched him go white around the mouth. "Then after that you'll kill any who step in the yard or on the property or in the county. Where's it going to end, friend? You want to be paid back for your arm? How many men do you figure it's worth?"

George Vale pushed his heavy voice between them. "I gave you an order, boy. Sit and eat or leave the room."

"Let him settle it," Talon said. "I'd as soon he did it now as to have to watch my back later." He slid his chair back and stood up. "As you can see, I left my sidearms to come to the table. That's a custom with me; I don't need a pistol to eat."

"I shoot no man in the back," Jonas Vale said. "And I won't stand and have any man say that I would."

"There doesn't seem to be much anyone says that you like too well, does there? Your father invites you to sit and eat, and you don't like that. You don't want your sisters to sit here. You don't like me or what I say. Now why don't you tell us what you do like, and then we'll try real hard to do it, and tonight you won't have to cry yourself to sleep because the mean old world hasn't been nice to you." He saw Jonas Vale tense, and the blood seemed to drain from his face; the urge to reach for one of his pistols was strong in his eyes, but he held himself back.

"You just can't do it, can you? Just can't draw a gun on an unarmed man." Ben let his expression soften. "It's hell to want to fight and not have anything to fight against. Now you know taking me on isn't going to help you one bit. You know I'm not scared of you. So you stop for ten seconds and think of just what you can win. You might give a thought to what you can lose. You're not dumb, friend. Two and two makes four to you the same as it does to me. So what about it?"

George Vale spoke quietly. "Your supper is getting cold, Jonas. And you're keeping our guest standing."

"I'll get you some fresh coffee," Emily said and got up from the table.

Jonas Vale let out a long breath and pulled back his chair and sat down. "As long as you're a guest here," he said, "I'll cause no trouble, but don't count on it another time, in another place."

"All right," Talon said. "I notice blood on your boots. You found where the hide hunters were working."

Jonas Vale nodded. "More than three hundred head skinned out." He looked at his father. "I want ten men and your permission to ride."

"Denied," George Vale said. "We'll start no war. That's my final word. You start it, Jonas, and you're through on this ranch."

Emily came back with another pot of coffee and poured a cup for her brother before sitting down. George Vale went on, "It's a rotten feeling for a man to have—to know that he can't do anything and that no one else will do anything, either."

"If they took one branded hide," Talon said, "the Army would move in. You could brand, Mr. Vale. At least you'd establish ownership."

"I've got twelve men on this place," he said, shaking his head. "I should have eighty. And I can't pay the twelve I have. They stay because they have no place else to go, and as long as I manage to feed 'em and give 'em a roof over their heads, they'll stay."

"I'd round up and brand," Ben Talon said again. "You don't have any choice, the way I see it. And after I'd made my gather, I'd hunt up this fella Goodnight, and I'd drive to market."

"Where is the market?" Jonas Vale asked. "I've talked to Goodnight, and even he doesn't know where the railhead really is. He heard it was in Kansas, but he's not sure. It's too big a risk."

"Risk what?" Talon asked. "Sit here and you'll lose cattle to the hide hunters. Drive and you may lose 'em on the trail, but that way you'll at least lose while doing something." He hunched his shoulders and put his elbows on the table. "First off, no one has any money, so hiring men to round up and brand is foolish to talk about. So don't talk about it. Talk survival to 'em. Make 'em understand that if you win and make it to market, then they'll get paid. Put it on the jaw-bone, as we say in the Army. Mr. Vale, when it comes down to it, you're forced to drive whether you like it or not and whether you believe it or not, and it doesn't make any difference if Goodnight knows what he's talking about. You sit here and you'll lose everything, a piece at a time maybe, but you'll lose it all just the same."

Jonas Vale said, "Yankee, I'm glad I didn't shoot you. That's what I've been sayin' for months now."

"Yes, it all sounds like the right thing to do," George Vale admitted. "And I've discussed it with the others, but we always run into a wall. Who's going to pay for the grub for so many men?"

"I'd eat beef three times a day if I had to," Talon said. "I'd collect potatoes and greens and flour from everyone who could spare a bushel or a cupful. I wouldn't sit on my—I wouldn't just sit."

"You're a tough man," Vale admitted, "but it's easier to be tough when you have money in your pocket."

"That's so," Talon said, reaching into his shirt for a small leather purse. He dumped about ninety dollars in coins on the table. "That's what's left of three months' pay. With beans at four dollars a bag and flour selling for two and a half, that ought to take a hundred men nearly a hundred miles."

"We don't take charity," Jonas Vale snapped.

Ben Talon looked at him steadily, and the young man grew nervous. "Now don't show me how stupid you can be," Talon said. He bowed to the housekeeper. "I enjoyed the meal and the company; thank you." Then he looked at Emily. "Would you care for a walk? It's early."

"Now see here—" Jonas said, then closed his mouth and looked at the tablecloth.

Color was high in Emily Vale's face, but she stepped outside with him, and they walked slowly away from the porch. "My," she said, "you're as bold as brass. I do declare, I think Jonas nearly choked." Then she looked at him and laughed. "It's been three years since a man called on me. I do think I like it."

"Three years? That's not easy to believe."

"Three years since a gentleman called," she said. "Does your arm bother you?"

"Only if I bump it," Talon said. He stopped by the horse corral and leaned against it so he could face her, look at her. There was a quarter moon and a bit of a chill to the wind. "Cold?"

"No. Ben, you didn't come out here because I dared you, did you?"

"I came to see you," he said. "You don't believe that?"

"I don't think you ever do anything for just one reason. What does it matter to you what happens to the Vales?"

"Don't you want it to matter to someone?" He took out his pocket watch and popped the case. "I was going to stay the night, but I think I'll make a long ride of it back." He put his watch away and touched her face; then he bent and gently kissed her. "Good-bye, Emily."

"Good-bye?"

"For a while," he said. "Just for a while."

"I don't understand you, Ben. I just don't."

"There's not much to understand. Come on, I'll walk you back to the house." He took her arm and turned her; he said good-bye again at the porch, then got his horse and rode out.

Major Bolton was napping in his office when Ben Talon returned; Ben had camped the night on the prairie and reached the post in midafternoon. There was a drizzling rain smearing the windows of Bolton's headquarters building, and Talon stoked the fire, and the noise woke the major. He yawned and stretched and scratched his stomach.

"Any trouble?" Bolton asked.

Talon shook his head; he went to the door to throw out the old coffee and grounds and make some new. "Vale may spend the fall and winter rounding up and branding; I think I've convinced him of that."

"Well, that's something," Bolton said. He lit a cigar and puffed it gently so the smoke wouldn't bite his tongue. "Did you mention the drive?"

"Yes. He may throw in with Goodnight. The boy wants to. I think he has more influence on the old man than meets the eye. I ran across the hide hunters. Young Vale said they got nearly three hundred head."

Harry Bolton nodded. "That's about the count that was brought to me late last night when Scully and Field brought the hides to Blaine's place." He got up and walked to the window and stared out at the gray day. "How did Blaine make his connection with the renegades? Scully? Field?"

Ben Talon shrugged. "I don't know, sir. I don't think Amy Leland had anything to do with it."

"Is that a fact or a guess?"

"Hunch," Talon said. "There's nothing wrong with hauling Blaine's hides, major. Hell, it's pure business with her. Just freight, that's all."

"Maybe that's right," Bolton admitted. "But with the police on the lookout for the renegades, they've made themselves mighty scarce, and I know they wouldn't have let Taylor Blaine get near enough to make them a proposition. If he had a friend, someone local here the renegades trusted —" He clamped his teeth into the cigar and left the sentence unfinished. "There's talk going around that Blaine is willing to pay a dollar a hide. It's only a matter of time before these ranchers like Vale and Early and Kirby take him up on it. A man can stay broke just so long—then he's got to do something about it, steal if he has to." He turned his head and looked at Ben Talon. "How does George Vale feel about the hide hunters?"

"He's holding himself back, but it's an effort. The boy wants to ride on the hunters, but the old man's put his foot down. How long, though, is a big question."

"I don't want to see it start," Bolton said softly. "I dread it, Ben."

Scully and Field were in back of Blaine's place, backed up by the warehouse door, their wagons staggering under a load of baled hides. Two of Blaine's men were counting and inspecting the hides while a crew of Mexicans unloaded and four hunters lounged against the wall of the building, enjoying a common jug of whiskey.

The going and coming of the hide wagons was so common a thing now that no one in town paid any attention, and if they noticed that a few of the renegades came in for liquor and supplies, they made a point of not talking about it. After all, they were really good Texans, just unfortunate in getting off on the wrong foot a few years back during the war when their raids in the name of the Confederacy began to lose patriotic fervor and become outright looting for profit. But they were all good men now, working for a living, and many in town envied them for the money they made—those good Yankee dollars.

The arrival of Owen Kirby, along with three wagons burdened with hides and flanked by ten of his men, did cause a stir along the street, and when it turned into the alley, everyone stopped working and watched them pull up and stop.

This ceasing of effort was immediately detected by Taylor Blaine, and he left his office and walked to the back loading platform. Owen Kirby was there, sitting his horse.

"I've brought you some hides," he said. "A hundred and fifty."

"And I'll buy them," Blaine said, his manner friendly. He did some mental arithmetic. "That comes to thirty-seven dollars and fifty cents."

Color climbed into Kirby's face. "It was my understandin' that you'd go a dollar a hide."

"That's a rumor," Blaine said. "I gave you my price the day I met with you in the office."

Owen Kirby stared at the man, and his temper, long strained without relief, broke completely. "I came for a dollar, and I'll get it!" he yelled and reached for his rifle.

One of the renegades, the one with the jug, dropped it and it broke; then he had his .44 Starr in hand, and it boomed. Owen Kirby dropped the rifle half drawn from the scabbard, clutched his chest, and rolled from the saddle.

He had barely hit the ground before his riders, weapons in hand now, opened fire. The renegades scattered, and bullets thudded into the wall where they had stood. One cried out and went into a tumble, legs and arms flailing; he fell loosely and lay still, staring at the sky.

The Mexicans dove under the wagons, and Blaine dashed inside and closed the door. Scully had his rifle into play now and shot one of Kirby's riders from the saddle before he was cut down himself and fell off the wagon.

The firing suddenly stopped, for the renegades had vanished, and the mounted men milled around, looking for targets, reloading their guns while two quickly dismounted and looked to Owen Kirby.

He was alive, and a cry went up, and they tore off a wagon seat and carried him down the street to the doctor's home. The doctor made them wait outside, on the lawn, while he had his look, and a half hour later he came out.

"The bullet's out," he said. "He may live. If he makes it

through the night—" He shrugged and went back in and closed the door.

The men decided to wait it out at the saloon, but it was boarded up; they walked on down to Dan Canby's store and filed in and bellied up to the counter.

Canby waited on them, setting out two bottles and tin cups. "I heard shootin'," he said. "Then I saw you carrying Owen Kirby—"

"Yeah, yeah," one man said. "So you saw it. You've got good eyes."

Canby stared at him. "Now don't get sore at me, friend."

"Then mind your damned store," the man snapped. "If Owen makes it, we'll be leaving town, no fuss. But if he don't, we're going to burn that Yankee carpetbagger to the ground."

"Now that doesn't sound very sensible," Canby said cautiously.

"Who the hell said it did?" another man asked.

Canby knew the extent of their temper. He said, "Help yourself to cheese. I've got some books to tend to." He smiled and went back, stopping and turning when he reached his door. "Sorry about Owen. He was a nice man. Tough, but nice." Then he stepped into his room and closed the door.

Taylor Blaine whirled, his expression slack with fear. "Pull yourself together," Dan Canby advised. "Keep your voice down. The walls are thin."

"My God, why did they come here?"

"To drink," Canby said. "You're safe enough if you keep quiet." He looked intently at Blaine. "You know, if you hadn't tried to rub Kirby's nose in it and make him sell for a quarter, none of this would have happened. Do you really know what it cost that man to slaughter cattle for the hides just to get enough money to feed his family? No, you don't know, and you don't give a damn."

"I didn't think he'd go wild," Blaine said. He sat down and clasped and unclasped his hands. "If he dies, will they burn my place?"

"To the ground."

"You've got to stop them. Where's the law?"

"What law?"

"The police."

"By the time they got here, it would be too late."

"The Army then," Blaine suggested. "I have a right to protection."

"Sure, but you'll have to do it yourself."

Blaine shook his head. "Canby, this means as much to you as it does to me."

"No it doesn't. I take my profit when I can, and I'm happy with what I get. If it ends, it won't mean a damned thing to me."

"But you're my partner, and—"

"I'm not your damned partner," Canby snapped. "And you say it again and I'll open that door and call Kirby's men. Now shut up. I'm going back out there."

When he came up to the counter, he put out another bottle. The men looked at it, and Canby said, "On the house." He counted noses. "Did someone leave?"

"Smoky. He went back to the doc's house to see how Owen was coming along."

Canby said nothing; he knew it was best to leave them alone. They remained in the store the rest of the afternoon and on into the evening. It was getting close to his closing time, but he held off saying anything about it.

Then Smoky came back, a runt of a man with no upper teeth. He simply shook his head, and all of them straightened up and stepped back from the bar.

One said, "I guess we know what to do now."

"Boys," Canby warned, "you're being fools."

"Then you better stay out of it," he was told, and the riders filed outside.

Dan Canby went to his front porch and stood there and watched them cross over and walk down to Blaine's place. They smashed the front windows and got in that way and broke the base of the lamps to get coal oil, and within a few minutes they had a half dozen fires going. Mounting flame began to brighten the street, and someone saw it and ran and rang the firebell. Then Smoky dashed out of the burning building and ran across toward Canby's store, carrying a large tin box.

He set it down on the porch and said, "There's the carpetbagger's money box." He pointed to the lock; it had been pried open. "We took a hundred and fifty dollars."

"You shouldn't have done that, Smoky."

"A man gets what he comes after, or he shouldn't bother with it," he said. The other riders were bringing up the horses, and they waited until Smoky mounted up. People were out on the street now, but they hung back, not sure of what was happening. Then when the men rode out of town, the fire brigades were formed, and they tried to save the adjoining buildings.

It was too late to save Taylor Blaine's place.

Canby went inside and locked his store, blowing out the lamps.

Blaine was pacing back and forth; when Canby opened the door he wheeled and pointed a small pepperbox pistol at him. "Put that stupid thing away," Canby said. "Well, they've burned your place. That was the fire bell you heard."

"Why? Because I wouldn't pay a dollar?"

"Blaine, don't you understand anything? I'd get out if I were you."

"No. I'm going to fight. I can, you know. And I will."

Canby shook his head. "That would be the wrong thing to do." He nodded toward the front of his store. "One of them came over with your money box. They took out the hundred and fifty for the hides."

"So they robbed me, too."

"No, they didn't. Let it go. You got off cheap. And lucky."

Taylor Blaine was over his fright. "Let me tell you something, horse trader. They've started something with me they'll wish they'd never thought of. When I'm finished, they'll be sorry they didn't give me the hides."

7

Amy Leland slapped her hand down hard on the desk top. "I will not haul one more bale of hides, and that is final!" Then she put her hands on her hips and looked at Dan Canby. He sat in an easy chair, one leg crossed over the other, a cigar drifting smoke past his fingers.

"Now why don't you be reasonable?" he asked. "Look, let me put it another way. You're in the stage business. A passenger puts down his money and is hauled from point A to point B and there are no questions asked. If the passenger turns out to be a bank robber, no one blames you because he got to town. Now it's the same with freight. A man pays his money and he's entitled to have freight hauled. It's not up to you to say what's hauled and what's not."

"How many men have you thrown out of your store and told never to come back?"

"Now, Amy, that's different. Those were always personal reasons. I still didn't stop selling food to his family."

"Owen Kirby is dead, and Scully is dead, and there's a full-scale war brewing, and I don't want to get caught in the middle of it." She waver her hand and sat down at her desk and leaned her elbow on it. "Dan, how did Taylor Blaine ever contact the renegades in the first place?"

"I did," he said frankly. "Blaine and I had a deal. I got a dollar a hide."

For a long moment she stared at him, then she slapped the desk again. "You're completely unscrupulous, aren't you?"

"Yes."

"You did it for money."

"Yes, and because someone was bound to do it. Even Kirby broke down and butchered for hides. It just had to happen sooner or later."

"Shooting? A war?" She shook her head. "Dan, you've got to take some of the blame for it. And so do I, for hauling Blaine's hides. I could have said no and put him out of business."

"But you didn't say no, and neither did I." He got up slowly. "We're partners, Amy. Let's not fight over this. Some time ago I came to the conclusion that I just couldn't keep everyone from sinking, so I've tried to save myself. Someone has to come out of this in halfway decent shape, and I figured that it might as well be me. I'd rather it was me than some Yankee. At least this money is staying in Texas."

"Oh, for Heaven's sake, Dan, stop moralizing!" She got up and walked up and down the room. "I feel like a vulture waiting for something to die. What's going to hold the Kirby place together now? If the farmers hear about it, they'll be swarming here, cutting it up with their fences and plows and—"

"You see? You know it's going to happen," Canby said. "Amy, sit down. Sit down and listen to me. If it's going to happen, then why don't *we* do something about it? At least have some control over it."

"What do you mean?"

"It would be better to pick the people who came here rather than take what comes." He gave his cigar butt a brief survey, then mashed it out. "Land development is a part of banking, and I own the bank. It only makes good sense to bring in farmers before squatters arrive."

"I can't believe I heard you right," Amy said. "Dan, I don't want any part of it!"

He shrugged. "I've made up my mind; it's an opportunity a man just can't pass up. I'll make loans, with their proved-up sections as security. It's just good business."

"Then let someone else have it," she snapped.

"That's not very realistic at all," Canby told her. "Amy, you've always had a lot of vision, and you weren't afraid to gamble. Go with me on this."

"Why? You don't need me. I've served my purpose, Dan."

"Amy, don't talk like that. I've always wanted to think that someday we'd be more than business partners. In a few years I'd like to go into politics; we're going to need influential men with money in this state. I want you with me all the way, Amy."

She watched him a moment, then said, "Do you want to buy me out, Dan?"

"No, I'd rather marry the business. I thought you'd guessed that."

"Of course; I'm not a fool, Dan. But what do you want? What are you after? I just don't know." She clasped her hands together and seemed very disturbed about it.

"My father left a peddler's wagon and two very tired horses when he died," Canby said. "I used to ride around the country with him while he sold pots and cloth and trinkets. That was my education, Amy, to add and work figures in my head. I learned how to horse-trade and always make a profit, because if I didn't, I'd go hungry. One day near Jefferson I got a wagonload of green peaches cheap. So I loaded the wagon with straw, wet it down, and covered my peaches; then I drove west, hardly stopping, keeping the straw damp during the hot days, and I sold those fresh ripe peaches for ten times what I'd paid for 'em. That's where I got the money to rent my store." He shrugged. "I made it pay by hiring no one, just working it myself, sixteen hours a day, seven days a week. When I enlarged it, I did most of the work myself to save the money. Some men spend their time looking for a woman or at the sunset or over the next hill. I've searched for opportunity, Amy. I've wooed it more steadfastly than a man ever wooed a woman. I don't know what I'm after. Not just a pile of money. Hell, I don't hoard it, Amy. I use it. Build with it. And I'm not saying that I know what's good for Texas or what's bad. But I do know that we just can't sit here in grinding poverty. Someone has to move, to change, to do something, and it takes money. Either my money or some Yankee's money." He shook his head. "No, I don't want you to buy me out, Amy, and I don't want to buy you out."

"I'm not going to haul hides," Amy Leland said.

"Yes, you are, because you're in the freight business. All

right, so the money isn't as clean as you'd like it, but it's still money, good Yankee gold, and you pay your teamsters with it, and they raise their families with it, and you buy harness and equipment. That may not be ideal or even what you want, but it's money, a living where there isn't any other."

"Don't you think I've thought about it?"

"If you have, then I know you'll do the right thing," Dan Canby said. "I've got to get back to the store. Blaine's gone out to see the major this morning. He wants protection so he can rebuild his warehouse."

"Why, the fool! They're apt to burn it down again."

Canby laughed. "Sure, but it'll take lumber and labor, and he'll support a payroll for three weeks while he's building. That's what I'm thinking of—work and wages. We need a lot of that, Amy. A man has to have work and the pay for it, or pretty soon he loses sight of the fact that he's a man."

"Dan, I don't think I'll ever understand what you really are, saint or sinner."

"I can give you one squad and no more," Major Bolton said firmly. He sat behind his desk, erect in the chair, hands wide apart on the desk top. "Blaine, I'm not at all in sympathy with what's been stirred up."

"Major, I'm in a legitimate business, and I have a right to protection under the law. Since there are no locally constituted authorities—"

"Yes, yes." The major waved his hand. "You'll get protection. I'll have a squad escort you back to town." He sighed and put a match to his dead cigar. "Now, about this letter. Surely you don't want to push this matter."

"My property was destroyed and money taken from me," Blaine said. "I certainly do wish the matter pursued. I've learned the identity of the men involved, and I want them posted and arrested as soon as possible."

"Mr. Blaine, I cannot stop you from this course of action, but I can appeal to your good sense and hope you will be persuaded to change your mind. I'm here to establish government and some stability of economy. You're here to make money for your company. Let me point out that employing the renegades to gather hides was not exactly a moral thing to do."

"But perfectly legal," Blaine insisted. "The cattle were unbranded and on open range. The fact that these men are ruffians who spent the war raiding their own people is no concern of mine."

"Mr. Blaine, these men are all kin of someone around here; they have families and brothers and parents still living here, kin who have turned them out, disowned them. To have employed them as you did aroused a good deal of resentment. Did you know that one of Owen Kirby's sons was in the renegade bunch? That's right. Kirby had turned him out some three and a half years ago because the boy wouldn't go and fight for the South; he'd rather remain in Texas and raise hell." He held up his hand when Blaine tried to speak. "I believe I can persuade the Kirby riders not to molest you further. But to prevent any further occurrence you will have to offer these ranchers a fair price for hides in the event they want to sell."

"And who pays for my building? And the hides I had stored there?"

"Kirby paid with his life. Can't you let it go at that?"

"No, I can't. Major, I'm responsible to my father and brothers. They would, I assure you, definitely not understand my doing nothing. Now, I've lodged a formal complaint with the military government. I expect that it will be processed and these men put on the wanted criminal list."

"All right," Harry Bolton said. "But I believe you're making a very big mistake."

"It's my decision. Now, if your soldiers are ready, I'd like to return to town and begin a new structure. This time I'm going to build out of adobe and fortify it. A man has the right to protect his property."

They met at George Vale's place because it was more centrally located than Fred Early's or Owen Kirby's. Nearly a hundred and fifty men crowded the yard while Vale and Early and their kin sat on the wide veranda.

Jonas Vale seemed to head up the younger men, and when he acted as their spokesman, no one objected. "I don't like to blame a dead man for anything, but Kirby played a fool's hand when he went for a shoot-out with Blaine's bunch. Those renegades wouldn't be cleaning the range now if we'd sold to Blaine in the first place."

"Not at twenty-five cents a hide," Fred Early said. "He doesn't need our hides now. That's why he offered Kirby a quarter."

"He'd need us if the renegades were driven out," Jonas said, waving his hand to include those standing in the yard. "And they'd ride with me."

One of the men standing in the front row nodded; he was dressed in faded, patched jeans, and the heels of his boots were run over. "Mr. Vale, I've got a cousin on my wife's side ridin' with the renegades, and their kids wear new jeans, and they put somethin' on their table 'sides beef and grits. It kind of makes a man think twice."

"He's right," another said. "Mr. Vale, we all know there ain't goin' to be any cattle drive till spring. So we're all in for a cold, lean winter. If them renegades was out of here, Blaine would have to pay a decent price or he just wouldn't buy any hides. Me'n my wife already lost one young un this summer when her milk dried up, and—well, I'm with Jonas. We all are, Mr. Vale. We just can't wait, 'cause we can't hang on."

"Have you thought what this can cost you?" George Vale asked. "A lot of you are going to get hurt. Some killed."

They knew that, and he knew that they knew it, but as the man had said, they were about used up, and when a man gets that way, even the big chances seem small. They weren't weak; they could take nearly anything, but it got to them when their wives and children suffered.

Fred Early said, "I've got sixty men who're ready to ride. How many do you have, George?"

"About that," Vale said.

"And there's thirty from Kirby's outfit," Jonas put in. "Why do we want to waste time?"

"Yes," the old man said, "now that we've decided, I think it's best that we move. Early will lead his men. How many are here from the Kirby outfit?" There was a forest of hands raised. "Will you men accept the leadership of my son Jonas?" They nodded, and the matter was done. "You can remain here for the night. Camp by the well and in the grove. We'll try to feed you." He got up. "Fred, Jonas, come inside. I have a map there, and we can work out the details."

They followed him into his parlor, and he spread the map on the table. "Most of the renegades camp in the vicinity of Oak Creek; they can roam unmolested in that area and on north fifteen or twenty miles. Some of them have settled down on small parcels of land there. Early, I suggest that you leave around dawn with your men. Strike in a northerly direction and make a day of it, then around sundown swing west and continue until it's dark. Camp the night there. Jonas, remain here until noon or a little after, then move west and see if you can find where their main camp is. Remain under cover and wait until well after dawn before striking. By that time I'll have taken my men around to the south, and we'll catch them no matter which way they run."

It sounded agreeable to them; they nodded, and Vale put his map away. "I'd as soon leave them alone; time and the law are going to break them up. But at a time like this, a man just can't think of himself. Now if you'll excuse me, I'll see if the help can come up with a meal for everyone."

Three soldiers and a sergeant got into an argument in Dan Canby's store, which ended when Canby threw them out, but not before they had broken a showcase and ruined some merchandise. Major Bolton, wishing to settle these matters justly and quickly, sent Sgt. Ben Talon in to make an estimate and sign a voucher so Canby could be paid.

It was a little after seven when Talon reached town and tied up in front of the store. Canby was alone, getting ready to close the store, when Talon walked in.

There was still some glass on the floor, small shards that crackled dryly beneath Talon's boots. "The major sent me to adjust the damages," Talon said. "If you could give me some idea—"

"Two table lamps, a case of chimneys, and a bolt of cotton print that got coal-oil-soaked. And the showcase."

"How much?"

"About a hundred dollars," Canby said.

"That sounds about right," Talon said and began to fill out the pay voucher.

"What do you know about storekeeping or prices?" Canby asked.

"Nothing. But I've got a good ear for what sounds right." He signed it and handed it over. "Any time you're at the post, present that and you'll be paid."

"Suppose I rode out tonight?"

Talon shrugged. "The sergeant of the guard would wake the officer of the day, who'd wake Major Bolton, who'd pay you and mumble at the inconvenience."

"The stuff wasn't broken at my convenience," Canby said. "I'll go out tonight before someone changes his mind."

"That's not very likely," Talon said.

"Just your word for that," Canby said and began to snuff out the lamps. Talon waited on the porch, and Canby went out and down the street to get his horse. A few minutes later he left town, taking the post road.

Ben Talon's first thought was to catch up with Canby, then he decided to walk down to the freight office and see what Amy Leland was doing. He saw the lights in her quarters and knocked, and she came to the door with a shotgun in her hand.

"Oh, it's you," she said.

"Now there's a greeting to stir a man's soul," Talon said, stepping in so she could close and lock the door.

"How was your visit to the Vales'?"

"Very nice," he admitted. "Did I detect a note in your voice—"

"Don't be ridiculous. I don't care what you do."

"Are we going to stand here or go sit in your parlor?" He watched her, and when she turned, he followed her and settled himself in a large horsehide-covered chair. With his good hand he lifted his arm from the sling and placed the elbow on the chair arm. "The major tells me that Blaine is going to rebuild. Adobe this time."

"Does the major tell you everything, Ben?"

"Just about. We've known each other a long time, and he knows that when I lost my commission, I didn't lose my brains at the same time. You knew that Blaine has had Kirby's men posted on the wanted list. The police are going out there tomorrow to see who they can arrest."

"I didn't know that," she said. "What a shame! He ought to know better."

"He does, but he wants to stay in business. A good way to do it is to scare trouble away."

"That won't work here. Everyone has had too much trouble to be afraid of a little more. Can I get you some coffee?"

"If it's already made. Don't go to any trouble for me."

"That's a strange thing to say." She poured a cupful and gave it to him. Then she sat down across from him and folded her hands over a raised knee. "I was thinking the other day that I'd like to go horse hunting or something."

"Alone?"

"Now you know I didn't mean that."

He shook his head. "Those days are gone for you, Amy. You're in a position to hire it done now. It's only when you're struggling hard that you really have any fun. Unfortunately, too few people realize that until it's too late. I knew a fella once, a miner. Hunted for eighteen years before he hit it rich. He always cooked his own meals, washed his own clothes, hunted his own food. Then he hired it done. Servants did everything. Finally he got disgusted and bought a boat, figuring he'd just sail away from it all, but he even had to have someone sail it for him. Got to the point where he couldn't do anything for himself, and he kept getting unhappier until finally he shot himself."

"Ben Talon, that whole story is a lie."

"Well, but it does illustrate a point, doesn't it?"

"I still cook for myself," Amy said. "I still run things."

"But it's slippin' away from you. Two bookkeepers now. Next month a manager, then a servant. Remember what I told you."

She let the gaiety leave her face. "Ben, what are you saying I should do?"

"Be happy, I guess. You're not."

"Yes, I am."

"Happy with the way things are going? Happy with Dan Canby?" He shook his head. "You don't fool me, Amy. You don't like what happened in back of Blaine's place. You don't like what Blaine is doing. But how do you pull in your oar, Amy?"

She let out a long breath. "I don't know, Ben. Do you?"

"Not unless it's buying or selling to Canby. He's the only one who has the money. But I don't think he—" He stopped talking and cocked his head to one side. "Was that someone at the door?" He got up and took a lamp with him and went to the door. Then he opened it and shined the light in Emily Vale's face; she quickly pushed it aside and stepped in where she couldn't be seen.

"Is Amy Leland here?" she asked.

Hearing her name, Amy came from her room. She looked at Emily Vale for a moment, then said, "What is it, Emily? What do you want here?"

"I was looking for Dan Canby."

"Why would you think he was here?"

"Why, I—" Emily Vale looked at Ben Talon, then shook her head; she didn't want to answer. "I've got to see Dan Canby right away. His store was locked, and no one seemed to know where he went, so I came here. You're his partner. Perhaps you'll give him a message."

"What is the message?" Amy asked.

"My father and brother and Fred Early are going to go into the Oak Creek country after the renegades. Dan knows how to reach them. They've got to be warned." She looked from Ben Talon to Amy Leland. "Please help me. Give Dan the message as quickly as you can. I've got to get back before I'm missed."

"I'll ride with you," Talon said.

"Oh, no, it's too far. It'll be near dawn before—"

"That's all right," he said. "I'll get my hat." He went back into Amy Leland's parlor and got his hat. When he came back, Amy was alone.

"She certainly doesn't have to whistle very loud, does she?" Amy said dryly.

"Do you really think it's that way?"

"You don't show me differently," Amy said.

He had no intention of arguing with her; he nodded and went outside for his horse. Emily Vale was waiting in the thick shadows, and they left town together, and for better than a mile there was no talking.

They they walked and led the horses. Talon said, "What does it matter to you what happens to the renegades?"

"Tom is with them—my younger brother. I don't want him dead."

"Do you think your dad or Jonas does?"

"I don't really know, and because of that, I'd rather see the whole bunch get away than run the risk." She turned her head and looked at him. "You think that's wrong?"

"Who am I to say? What relationship does Dan Canby have with—"

"He's always helped them when he could, even during the war. Some say that Dan Canby made his first big money when he'd sell a barrel of flour to a man, then tell the renegades so they could steal it back, and he'd sell it over."

"Somehow that sounds like him," Ben Talon admitted. "Yet you went to him."

"There was no one else. Tom and I have met on the prairie. He's told me about Canby, bringing them supplies and working with them. It was Canby who got them to work for Blaine. The two of them have some kind of deal."

"That sounds like Dan, running after a dollar." He stopped and boosted her on her horse, then mounted his own. "How did you sneak out of the house without waking your sisters or the housekeeper?"

"Oh, the housekeeper left three days ago to visit her sister who lives over by Fort Graham. My sisters went with her, and they won't be back for a month."

"If you get tired, we can stop awhile, Emily."

"I—don't think I should, Ben. It wouldn't be right, us alone like this."

"Are you afraid?"

"Kind of. But I don't know what of. I don't know my feelings, Ben. I just don't."

"I kissed you once, and you didn't mind."

"You think I've forgotten? Let's go on."

8

BECAUSE SHE was really too tired to go on and wouldn't admit it, Ben Talon made Emily Vale dismount, and he built a fire and made her roll up in his blankets and sleep for a while. Her protest was a token; she was worn to a frazzle, and she went to sleep immediately while he sat by the fire and kept his rifle handy. Aside from not wanting to have her ride this lonely distance alone, Ben Talon hoped to reach the Vale place in time to keep the men from riding on the renegades.

It just wouldn't do to start a fight that would get brother firing on brother and the whole country in an uproar. They had more trouble than they could handle, but it was the way with people to always ask for more. It seemed like the more trouble they had, the more they wanted. Trouble addled the mind, it seemed. It made a sensible man foolish, so that he compounded his mistakes until something brought him up short and forced him to think again.

Talon didn't doubt that George Vale wanted to do the right thing, but once the shooting began, the cowboys would get wild—not much at first, but wild—and the day would come when other law-abiding people would ride on them, for they'd become as bad as the renegades.

After letting her sleep for nearly two hours, Talon woke her, rolled his blankets, helped her on her horse. Then they rode on, reaching the Vale place a bit before dawn.

George Vale and his men were gone.

So was Fred Early.

Kirby's men were in the cook shack having their breakfast,

and Emily dismounted and went around to the side of the house without anyone noticing her. As soon as she was out of sight, Ben Talon started whistling as he tied up, and Jonas Vale came out.

"What are you doin' here?" he asked.

"Happened to be in the vicinity." He turned his head and looked at the cook shack. "Gettin' an early start, ain't you?" He looked at Jonas. "The sky's just turning gray. You already eaten?"

"I didn't feel like it this morning," Jonas said. "Fact is, I don't feel none too good. Come on in, now that you're here. I'll have the help bring you breakfast."

"Coffee will be fine," Talon said, stepping inside. "Early and your father have already gone, huh?"

Jonas Vale looked at him. "How did you know about it?"

Talon shrugged. "Told you I was just riding around. You pick up things that way. Nothing people say, but what they don't—it all added up to a raid on the outlaws." He followed Jonas into the kitchen. "It's a damned-fool move, you know."

"But we're going to make it," Jonas said. His eyes were bright, and there was a pronounced flush to his cheeks; Talon noticed this as he sat down.

"You'll do better for yourself and for all of you if you ride back to see Goodnight and tell him you'll throw in with him in the spring."

"We'll be there," Jonas said. "You can bet on it. But now there's this business at hand." He cocked his head to listen to any sound in the other part of the house. "Wonder where Emily is. She's usually up about this time."

"What do you want her to do? Wave good-bye to you?"

Jonas Vale didn't get offended. "When I leave, Talon, you stay here."

"I thought I'd go along. When you get through with this fool's play, someone ought to be around who has the straight of it and whose judgment wasn't colored by bad temper." He studied Jonas carefully. "You know, you don't look well. What's the matter?"

The young man shook his head. "It came on me last night; I threw up my supper. Toward morning I was running a little fever. Probably something I picked up in Goodnight's camp. The damned fools over there don't know enough to wash pots and pans. But I'll be all right."

"Why don't you call it off? You've got an excuse."

Jonas Vale laughed. "Mister, if I was leaking blood, I'd ride when the time came."

There was no use arguing with him, and Talon knew it; Jonas was determined to go through with this. Talon wondered where Early and the old man were, then decided that they were riding in a circular direction, meaning to close in from the sides while Jonas and his men made the actual attack. There really couldn't be any other reason.

Talon finished his coffee and said, "When are we leaving?"

"Later. Around noon. Do you want a fresh horse?"

"No, I'll do with my own."

He went out under the shade trees and slept for several hours; then the cold wind cut him deeply, and he got up and walked around the yard. There wasn't going to be much of a sun; the sky was solid overcast, and the temperature was down in the forties, pushed by wind.

It was his intention to take his noon meal in the cook shack, but Emily came to the porch and motioned for him to come inside, and he went with her to the kitchen. Jonas Vale was not around, and before he could comment on it, she said, "He's not feeling well, so he went to his room to sleep." She pulled back a chair and put a plate of eggs and potatoes before him. "I wish we had more, Ben."

"Why, this is just fine." He waited while she sat down across from him.

"I was thinking of what I said to you the first time I saw you, and I'm ashamed."

He shook his head. "Now don't be. People have to get to know each other, Emily."

Someone came in the house and stopped in the kitchen doorway; he was one of Kirby's men. "Jonas ready to ride?"

"He's in his room," Emily said. "Down the hall and on the right at the end." The man left, and she looked at Ben Talon. "You're going, too?"

"Yes."

"You won't be able to stop it, Ben."

"Well, I've got to try."

"Don't get hurt doing it. None of them are worth it, really."

Jonas Vale came into the kitchen and filled a sack with biscuits and cold meat; he was sweating slightly, and his face was flushed. To Ben Talon he said, "If you're going, let's go," and then went out, the Kirby man following him.

"I guess it's time," Talon said, rising. Emily came around the table and put her arms around him and kissed him, and he held her for a moment, then stepped back. "Now that was sure nice," he said.

"Ben, will you watch over Jonas for me?"

"Why, sure." He patted her cheek, then picked up his hat and coat and went outside where the others were getting ready to mount up. He untied his horse, swung up, and sided Jonas Vale as they left the yard.

All the rest of that day they moved southwest across rolling land with the grass bent down by the wind, and come sundown the cold was biting through their coats, and now and then a man would blow on his hands and wish he'd brought gloves along. They made cold camp along a timbered creek, and Jonas Vale's teeth were chattering, and he wouldn't eat anything at all.

It was a miserable night, and they remained until nearly midnight, then got ready to move on. One of Kirby's riders tried to get Jonas Vale out of his blankets, but the young man was too sick to move.

Ben Talon went over to see what he could do; he felt of Vale's face and found him burning with a high fever. To one of the Kirby men he said, "Get a fire going."

"It might be seen."

"What the hell does it matter? He's not going on. He can't."

"Guess you're right there," the man said, and they began to gather brush. Soon they had a fire blazing, throwing out a wide circle of light.

The man named Smoky seemed to be in charge of the Kirby men; he came over and looked at Jonas Vale for a long time. "If I didn't know better, I'd say it was smallpox." Then he laughed at the hush this brought. " 'Course it can't be. There's no smallpox around here."

"He ain't always been around here," another man said. "He's been over in the next county and then some, with that fella Goodnight."

That was enough to make them back up, but Ben Talon remained by Jonas Vale. "A couple of you men make a travois, and I'll take him into town to the doctor."

"If he's got smallpox, I wouldn't go takin' him into town," Smoky said. He turned to several men. "Cut some poles and fix a blanket for him." He stood with his lips pursed. "We've got to be gettin' on if we're to hit them renegades come dawn. It's another twenty miles."

"Then go," Talon said. "I'll manage alone."

"Hate to leave you," Smoky said.

"Like hell," Talon said. "There ain't anybody man enough here to touch him." He looked around. "Go on. Lift him off his blankets. You? No? Go on then. Shoot yourself some renegades."

"Get the horses," Smoky said. Then he turned back to Ben. "Look, you already touched him. Ain't no sense to anyone else taking the chance of handling him. Besides, we got a job to do. Good luck there, Yankee."

"Oh, sure," Talon said and checked the travois that had been lashed together. They rode out, not wasting any time about it, and he managed to get Jonas Vale tied on. Then he mounted and swung east, dragging the travois behind him.

He couldn't really blame these men for deserting him. Smallpox was a thing that would drive fear into the bravest man, if that was what Jonas Vale had. And only a doctor could tell for sure.

To Talon's way of thinking, the stage station was the nearest, but there was no doctor there, and none within twenty miles. Town was his only bet, and there was a lot of open country yet to travel, and he couldn't go very fast; Vale was too sick for that.

So he turned almost due north and rode for better than two hours without stopping. The wind seemed to die down a little; he thought it was his imagination, but finally the night was still, and it grew warmer, so much so that he took off his coat and rode in his shirt sleeves.

He smelled the rain before it came, and this gave him time

to stop and dismount and untie his poncho. He covered Vale with it just as the rain began. It fell heavily, straight down, drumming the grass and soaking him thoroughly before he got mounted again.

The rain held steady until dawn, then when it grew daylight, it seemed to slack off a little, falling in a steady drizzle. It was nearly ten by his pocket watch when he saw Abilene off a bit to the right, and he changed course, riding on for another forty minutes before he reached the outskirts.

He saw a boy throwing rocks into a puddle near the end of the street. Talon whistled, and the boy came over. "Sonny, go fetch the doctor. This man's been hurt."

"Did you shoot him, mister?"

"Yes," Talon said. "Now will you get the doctor?"

The boy ran off down the street, and Talon got down from his horse, muscles in his back protesting. He waited for ten minutes, then the doctor came down the street, the small boy tagging behind.

"Why the hell couldn't you bring him into town?" the doctor asked as he came up.

"You take a look and you'll know," Talon said. "Go on home, sonny. And thanks."

"I want to stay," the boy said.

"You git on home," Talon said. "Go on now."

The boy turned and walked away, and Ben Talon stepped near the travois. "Do you know what ails him?" the doctor asked, looking up.

"Smallpox, I guess."

"That's right. Lord knows where he got it, but if word gets around—" He straightened. "There's an empty shack on the other side of town, near the stable. Take him there. Get him inside, then come to my office right away." He measured Talon with his eye. "Have you any money, sergeant?" He held out his hand. "I'll send someone for a complete change of clothes for you. I'll burn everything you're wearing."

Talon gave him thirty dollars in gold. Then he mounted and circled the town, coming in on the east side. He found the shack, opened the door, unlashed the travois, and dragged Jonas Vale inside. The bunk wasn't in good enough repair, so Talon left him on the floor and went out, closing the door the best he could.

The doctor was waiting for him at his office; he had a bath ready and gave Talon orders to scrub thoroughly with strong soap and disinfectant. By the time Talon was finished, the doctor was back with a bundle of clothes, and Talon began to dress.

"I'm going over to the shack," the doctor said. "I don't suppose there's any real hope of keeping this quiet."

"I guess you can't keep a thing like this quiet," Talon said. "Is he going to make it?"

The doctor shrugged. "Some do, but most don't. But if he dies, it will have to be alone. Everything he's touched will have to be burned. Where did you find him?"

Ben Talon told him the whole thing, and the doctor listened, his expression going more grave as Talon talked. "All right, sergeant, here's what you'll have to do. You'll have to burn that place."

"Vale's ranch house?"

"That's right. Get everyone who's been in there to burn their clothes and bathe as you did. But you've got to put a torch to that place and every other building he's been in. This spreads like a prairie fire, sergeant. I don't have to tell you that." He clapped Talon on the arm. "You look pretty frazzled, but you can't stop now. Get a belt of whiskey and a fresh horse and get going."

The rain had stopped by the time Ben Talon reached the Vale place; it was late afternoon, and Emily ran out as he got down. "Where's Jonas and the others?"

"The others went on," he said, leading her toward the porch. Then he told her where Jonas was and that he had smallpox. He thought she was going to cry, but he shook her, and she listened carefully to him. "I want you to think back. Remember if you've been in a room where Jonas was since you've come home."

She thought, then shook her head. "No. I went back to sleep after you left. No, I haven't, Ben."

"Jonas couldn't really have started being contagious until his fever climbed high," he said. "That was about the time we started out; I remember that he was sweating. Emily, we've got to burn the house and the bunkhouse if he's been there."

"Burn it? Oh, Ben, no!"

"I'm sorry, but it has to be. The doctor explained it to me. All of you who've been in the house will have to scrub good with strong soap and burn the clothes you had on. I've got to do that, Emily. Now will you help me?"

"Do I have to?"

"No, I can do it myself, but you've got to understand that I don't want to."

She thought about it, then nodded. "There's a cook and a servant; I'll tell them. What can we take, Ben? Anything?"

"Whatever you're positive Jonas has not touched. If he sat in a certain chair, you'll have to leave it. All right?"

"Yes."

Darkness seemed to come early because the day had been so gray. George Vale and the men following him stopped on the prairie because there was a glow ahead where his house should be, and he studied this a moment before he could accept the fact that his place was afire.

He was not in a position to travel fast for he had wounded with him, a dozen men on litters and twice that many riding, some lying on the horse's neck because they could no longer sit erect.

The renegades had hit them well after dawn, well after the time when Vale had expected them, and they had come on in a rush, shooting their way clear—not many, no more than forty or fifty. Vale's men had thinned them out considerably before the renegades broke into the clear and vanished in the gray vastness of the prairie.

Some of the bodies they buried in shallow graves, then the ground, muddy and hard to dig, discouraged them, and they left some on the prairie and rode toward home, winners, but having won nothing.

When Vale made out the fire, he and a half dozen men rode on ahead, punishing their tired horses, and they stormed into the yard as the beams smashed down and the heat-dried adobe cracked, letting part of one wall settle in a shower of sparks.

Talon and Emily and the few who had been left behind stood by the well, and Vale flung himself off his horse, roughly demanding, "What started it? In the name of God, what caused it?"

"I burned it," Ben Talon said, and the old man flung himself on him and would have struck him if Emily had not rushed in and grabbed his arms.

"Papa, listen! Papa, we had to ! Jonas has smallpox!"

The old man was instantly calm, instantly grave. "Where is my boy?"

"I took him to town," Talon explained and told him what happened at the night camp.

"So they went off and left him," Vale said. "I'll kill them all!"

He didn't mean it; Talon understood and ignored it. "Likely some of them are working up a fever or starting one, Mr. Vale. But I think we've checked it here. Emily, the cook, and the servant have thought about it real good, and we don't figure that Jonas has been any place but the house. If the men from the Kirby place didn't drink from his cup, they may have missed it." He looked at the men who had ridden in with George Vale and noticed that one of them had a bloody bandage on his upper arm. "So you found the renegades."

"They found us," Vale said. "They made one bolt through and left a lot of dead. They left half of their own, too." He wiped a hand across his mouth. "Smallpox. I wonder where he got it."

"The doctor thinks maybe over in the next county. Smoky thought so, too. Did you see any of Smoky's men?"

Vale shook his head. "Early, either. I don't know whether or not they reached the renegade camp. When the renegades hit us, they seemed just as surprised as we were. None of us expected 'em so early. More like midafternoon." He sat down and put his hands on his knees and looked at the ruins of his house and the furniture and piled goods out near the tool shed. "God, what else can go wrong?" He looked at Ben Talon. "Will you tell me that? What else can go wrong?"

When Hank Swain saw Barney Ryder fall as he tried to climb aboard the coach, Swain figured that Barney had forsaken the pledge, and he went out into the yard to fire him on the spot. But when he got near, he saw that Barney wasn't drunk; he was sick. The passengers got out of the coach and stared at the fallen man, and finally one of them thought to go fetch the doctor.

That afternoon three more took sick, and nearly everyone in town knew that it was smallpox.

Ben Talon returned to the post and brought Emily Vale with him; he saw that she was comfortable in one of the officers' vacant quarters, then went to post headquarters to see Major Bolton. Talon had been away for a week because he hadn't wanted to leave Emily until he was certain that she had not contracted the disease, and when he'd known for sure, he'd insisted that she come back with him.

Bolton was signing some papers when Talon came in; he sat down when Bolton waved him into a chair. Then the major finished and rubbed his palm against his unshaven cheek. "Three days since I've shaved. Not very military, is it?" He offered Talon a cigar. "Well, we've got a good one on our hands, haven't we? Six dead in town and half the population in isolation. I've sent both of the contract surgeons in to do what they can and sent a courier to fetch three more. How are things out on the prairie?"

"You wouldn't believe it, major. Smoky and the Kirby men raided the renegade camp after they'd pulled out. Helped themselves to what they wanted. The renegades were all sick with smallpox; some had already died."

"Good Lord!" Bolton said. "How did it start, Ben?"

"Well, I've been trying to put it together," Talon said. "I figure I have all the pieces by now. First off, I thought that Jonas Vale brought it in, but then he wasn't the first that took sick. Old man Vale found where his young son Tom had been buried, and from the condition of the grave at the renegade camp, he figures that he died ten days ago. That means that the renegades had it before Jonas did." He shook his head. "Now a couple of the stage drivers have it. That really confuses things. I'd like to know if Jonas ever rode the stage."

"Ask him," Bolton said. "He made it. Fever broke, and he's staying at the doctor's house. Weak, but he made it."

"Would you ride in with me, sir?"

"Yes. I could do with the change." He got up and told the orderly to have his horse brought around. "I've declared the town off limits; we'll try to keep the post clean. What are you thinking about, Ben?"

"If Jonas rode the stage, and any of the renegades rode the stage—"

"That's been my thought, too. The coaches could be carrying the damned stuff all up and down the line."

"Major, have you heard any word about whether or not the Indians have it?"

"To tell you the truth, my patrols haven't reported seeing Indians for a month." The orderly came in to say that the horse had been brought around, and the major and Talon went out together and mounted.

After they cleared the guard at the gate and rode on toward town, Bolton said, "I've been very reluctant to order property burned, but the doctor, backed by Dan Canby, has been setting fire to several buildings. Both the surgeons agree that this is the best way to halt it." He turned his head and looked at Ben Talon. "I'd hate to have to tell Miss Leland to burn her coaches and stations."

"It may come to that," Talon said. "And Blaine's new place, too. If the renegades had it and brought in hides to Blaine's place—"

"That's right; I've forgotten about him since I pulled the squad back to the post. We'll check on it before we leave town." He licked a cigar into shape, then cupped his hands around the match. "I've heard where whole towns went up in smoke before an epidemic was stopped. Hate to see it come to that. These people have lost a war, sons, money; they can take only so much, Ben."

9

AMY LELAND stared at them. "You want to burn my stages?"

Harry Bolton nodded gravely. "I'm sorry, but I see no other way. We've talked to Jonas Vale—he caught one of your stages near Cameron several weeks ago. At that time he noticed two men riding in the coach who were known to be part of the renegade gang. Now it's most likely that the two men Vale recognized were coming down with smallpox then and passed it on. Two of your drivers are down with it now, and there'll be more, and passengers who rode in those coaches."

"But to burn all of them—why, I'm out of business!"

Ben Talon said, "The stations, too, Amy." He took the cigar stub out of his pocket and threw it into the potbellied stove. "I've asked Dan Canby to come over here, since he's your partner. Amy, if there was any other way, don't you think we'd be glad to do it?"

"At any rate you're closed down for the time being," Major Bolton said. "I've already dispatched couriers south and north with orders for the police to stop the stages. At my surgeon's suggestion, I'm having notices sent to doctors from Fort Smith to Matamoras, asking them to contact anyone who has ridden on the line within the past ten days and isolate them for possible smallpox infection."

"You've just put me out of business," Amy Leland said flatly. Then she let out a long breath. "What does it matter? I'd have stopped the stages anyway."

Dan Canby came in and closed the door against the cold weather. He opened his coat and shook some heat inside.

"Just what's going on? I hear you're going to close up the town."

"A rumor without foundation," Bolton said, "but we are stopping everyone who tries to leave. And we're not allowing anyone to enter. I've just told Miss Leland that we'll have to burn her coaches and stations. We're certain that her stages transmitted the infection."

Canby looked steadily at him, then laughed. Ben Talon said, "You find this funny?"

"Burning the coaches and stations? You bet I think that's funny. Now you just try it, soldier, and you'll get hurt. We've got a fortune tied up—"

"We're talking about people's lives," Bolton said sternly.

"So what? They take a chance when they get on a horse. It's the same riding the stage." He shook his head. "Don't try to burn anything, major. I hope you've got sense enough to heed that warning."

"We'll start with the stages here in the yard," Bolton said. "Sergeant Talon, will you see that they are fired within the hour?"

"Yes, sir." Ben Talon brought his heels together and saluted with his left hand; his right, still bandaged, was tucked into his shirt because he still could not use it.

"Talon, don't put a torch to my property," Canby said. "I'll kill you if you do."

Amy Leland said, "Dan, the money can't be more important than—"

"It is!" he snapped. "I've got half the say around here, and there'll be no burning. No destruction of my property." He buttoned his coat and turned to the door. "I'm going to get my pistol, Ben. I'll use it on you if I have to."

He slammed the door on the way out. Bolton said, "You have the order, sergeant. Carry it out, using any means you find necessary."

"Yes, sir."

"Ben," Amy said, "God knows what's gotten into Dan. Be careful. And don't kill him."

"Not unless he makes me," Talon said and went out, tipping his head down against the rising wind. He went around the building to the wagon yard. Hank Swain was there as though he had a notion something bad was going to happen. Talon told him what had to be done, then he told Swain that, once the stages were wheeled close together, he was to get out of the yard.

"I seen Canby storm out," Swain said and turned, calling to a pair of Mexicans.

There was a five-gallon can of coal oil in the barn, and Talon got it. The coaches were being parked hub to hub, and he climbed up and began to pour coal oil over them, splashing it around. He emptied the can and threw it down; then he saw Dan Canby standing by the pole arch entrance, a pistol thrust into his waistband. Canby wore no coat or hat; he stood spraddle-legged, braced against the breeze.

"That's going far enough," he called against the wind. "Climb down or get shot off there, Ben."

Talon straightened. His pistol was tucked underneath his coat in a flap holster, and he knew that Canby would get off the first shot and that it would likely be a fatal one because Canby was what the Mexicans called a *pistolero*, a shooter with two gunfights behind him.

"I'm too good a target up here," Talon said and grinned and started to climb down, making a clumsy job of it. By the time he hit the ground, hidden by part of the coach, he had his coat open and the flap unfastened on his holster. He glanced at the barn and saw Hank Swain there. "Bring me a torch, Hank."

Then he waited while Swain wrapped a rag around a stick, soaked it in coal oil, and lit it. Swain carried it across the yard, all the time watching Dan Canby. Swain handed the torch to Talon, then ran for the barn. Talon held the torch away from him so that the heat and smoke didn't get into his eyes.

"If you throw that," Canby said, "you're a dead man, Ben. I don't want to kill you, but I will. You can't take this much from a man and not have him fight."

"We do what we have to do," Talon said and arched the torch on top of the nearest stage. He didn't wait to hear it land, but dropped and rolled. Dan Canby's bullet slivered wood near the driver's boot, and Talon was out of sight, his own .44 drawn now.

The coaches were beginning to burn; the flames spread quickly with great noise and a pall of dark smoke that billowed away between himself and Dan Canby.

Talon dashed across the yard and almost reached the barn door before Canby saw him and fired again. The range was more than sixty yards, and the bullet went a bit wide. Kneeling down, Talon raised his injured arm and planted it against the door frame. Then he laid the muzzle of his gun across his forearm, sighted, and squeezed off.

Dan Canby staggered, and one leg bent; he quickly clutched the upper thigh. He started to hop, stopping when Ben Talon yelled. "I could have put that one in your brisket, Dan! If I have to shoot again, I will!" He cocked the Remington and waited, squinting over the sights. Canby, hobbling, couldn't make cover ahead of another shot, and the man knew it. He hesitated only an instant, then dropped his Colt on the ground and sat down to try to stem the bleeding.

Talon left the barn, and Hank Swain and several others followed him over to where Canby sat. The wind husked dust and blew Canby's hair, and he looked at Talon, his expression tight because he was beginning to hurt a little now.

"Give him a hand there, Hank," Talon said. "Is this the end of it, Dan?"

"I don't know." He turned his head and looked at the coaches kind of melting together, collapsing, throwing out a strong heat. "If you only knew how hard they were to get and what they cost."

"Hell, man, I know."

Swain helped Canby stand; they started off down the street, Canby hopping along, throwing his weight onto Swain. Ben Talon picked up Canby's gun and stuck the long barrel in his waistband. One shot gone; that was really Canby's way: one shot, hoping to make the first one count.

Then he saw Amy Leland and the major standing in the back doorway; she was watching her coaches char to ruin. A hot rim, free from a burned-out wheel, rolled around the yard in ever smaller circles, then stopped, wobbling, in the dust, like some strange wounded bird in a death dance.

She turned and went inside, and Ben Talon went in, too. She was pouring coffee when he closed the door, and her eyes were red, but she wasn't crying, and he didn't think she would.

"I suppose I should be happy you didn't burn my freight wagons, too." She stared at her coffee cup a moment, then looked at Ben Talon. "When Dan went out there with his gun, I wasn't sure whether I wanted him to stop you or wanted you to not kill him. Do you understand how that could be?"

"Yes," he said and drank his coffee.

Presently she sighed and murmured, "I guess Dan's a strong-minded man, all right. I just didn't really believe he'd actually shoot at the Army to protect his property."

Ben Talon studied her a moment. The he said gently, "There's different ways of being strong-minded, Amy." And left it at that.

Bolton looked at his watch. "I think we'd better get over to Blaine's place." He sighed and put his watch away. "This is miserable work, Miss Leland. Just miserable." He put out his hand and touched her shoulder. "Perhaps, someway, somehow, we can replace part of the equipment you've lost. I don't know, but it's something we can hope for."

They left her building and walked toward town and Blaine's nearly finished building. His office was in front, but he was not there. He occupied a room for housekeeping, and Talon went toward the back of the building and found the door open.

One look was all he needed; Blaine was on his cot, his face broken out in pustules, and his eyes were glazed with fever. Talon closed the door and found Major Bolton waiting in front. "I'll go fetch the doctor," he said, nodding toward the back. "He's got it good."

"Well, that rather settles that, doesn't it?" Bolton said. "I'll wait here and make sure no one enters."

The first thaw came in March, and the weather turned mild for a change, and some of the more optimistic opined that a very bad winter was coming to an end.

For more than three weeks no one had come down with smallpox, and the doctor, who had aged five years in the past two and a half months, decided that it was possible that the epidemic had been checked.

But not without cost. The stages had been stopped for a

little over four months, and traffic in and out of town had come to a standstill. Smallpox had done what the police could not do, what Vale and Early and the others could not do; it had wiped out the renegades. All of them took sick, and those who survived took their scars and went home, hunting relatives who had once ousted them. Now there were no more renegades, just men back with families and having no more desire to go it alone, living alone, dying alone.

The smallpox killed the hide buying because, once recovered, Taylor Blaine hitched a ride on a northbound freight wagon and didn't bother to say good-bye to anyone.

Canby limped around for a while, but the bullet wound in his leg healed, and he stayed in town, stayed close to his bank. Once, when Ben Talon rode in, Canby stayed on one side of the street while Talon walked the length of the other; they were like fighting cocks, each unafraid but respectful of the spurs of the other.

Everyone in town knew that the smallpox had come in on Amy Leland's stages. Most understood that she wasn't responsible for that, but others who had lost loved ones felt that just burning her wagons wasn't enough, and there was talk going around that someone ought to burn her out instead of stopping with the stages.

But they never got around to it. News of the big cattle drive going north seemed to be on everyone's mind, and since Vale and Early were hiring hands, most of the young men in town left to join the drive. Amy Leland let them have four wagons, and these were loaded from Canby's store. Many people said that it was a real generous thing to do, while others thought that it was just Canby & Leland sticking their fingers into another money-making pie.

Some Army men came onto the post, having ridden down from Kansas, and they soon spread the word that the railroad was in Ellsworth and that the town was chock-full of cattle buyers just praying for a herd to come north and that the market was up to about thirty dollars a head. Of course, this was too late to pass on to Vale or Early or the others; they were already on the trail and didn't know exactly what to expect in Kansas.

But it didn't keep the people in town from doing some multiplication and figuring out that jointly Vale and Early were worth seven hundred and fifty thousand dollars, by the Ellsworth market. There was a lot of hand rubbing and lip smacking and talk about getting their credit extended at the bank and stores.

Spring brought new people to town, people with wagons and straw hats; the men wore overalls, and the wagons had a plow lashed onto the side, and these people had money. They stopped at Canby's and deposited their money and talked about land for sale, or land to homestead, or land to squat on.

They were all stern-faced, determined people who spoke in hard, Midwestern accents, stomping hard on the r's, pushing them into their noses so they twanged. They all had many children, and wives who didn't seem to like anything about Texas, and on Sundays they got together and prayed and sang loudly, and afterward they had a big feed, while the men sneaked off to nip at their jugs.

These people owned no cattle, just cows to be milked and pigs to root up the barnyard, and they fenced everything. The children immediately were put to work digging postholes and stringing single-strand wire and driving staples, and when they had fenced in the land they had bought or rented or squatted on, they fenced the barnyard, using wood, and then fenced the front yard and the back yard and put another fence up so they could keep chickens.

Ben Talon, who had been out of the county since late January, didn't get back until mid-May; he had been south, to Victoria, on special assignment, helping to reactivate the Texas Rangers. When he returned, he was surprised to find soddies and frame houses going up on creeks and around springs on George Vale's land.

As he approached one of these houses, the family came out to watch him, and he saw no display of weapons, but he noticed that the man stayed close to the open door, and Talon surmised there was a shotgun leaning there.

Talon's uniform was a help; it was blue, and Yankee, and these people expected no trouble from Yankees. He stopped and gave his horse some water, then tied him and walked toward the house. He introduced himself and shook hands with the man, who ignored his wife and seven children.

"It ain't much now," the man was saying, "but in another two or three years it'll be a nice farm."

"Guess you knew this land was all part of the Vale ranch," Talon said matter-of-factly.

"According to Mr. Canby, it's open range. It suits us fine. We'll be good neighbors to the Vales, although they ain't come around to bid us howdy."

"The old man and his boy and all of his riders are on a cattle drive to Kansas. But he'll be around when he comes back and hears you're here."

"Cattle drive to Kansas?" the farmer said. Then he laughed. "I never heard of such a thing. Why, it's too far. Any fool knows that." He let his laughter die to a chuckle. "How many head do they own, anyway?"

Talon thought a moment; he wanted to be honest. "About eighteen thousand head."

The man stared at him, his brow furrowed. "Don't lie to me, soldier. I'm not an idiot."

"Well, they left here in the spring, two outfits, with twenty-five thousand head between them," Talon said. "About two hundred riders, eight hundred head of horses, and four wagons. Believe it if you want to, but I'll tell you one thing you'd better believe: George Vale fought for this land, and he won't like to see you cut it up with a plow and muddy his creek. And if he calls on you to tell you to leave, he'll have seventy men riding with him, and I wouldn't stop to argue. I'd pack my things and get out."

"This land is as much mine as it is his," the farmer said.

"Well, that's your opinion," Talon said. "Hope you don't take it to the grave with you." He bowed to the wife and smiled at the children, then got on his horse and rode on.

Before he reached the Vale place, he saw three more farms.

It was dusk when he rode into Vale's yard. Another house had been built, a much smaller house, and as he tied his horse, Emily came out, then ran to him and flung her arms around his neck. A crippled horse wrangler, one of the five men who remained behind, found this too much to take—a fair Southern woman hugging a Yankee—and retreated to brood about it.

They went into the house; Emily had been fixing supper,

and she put on another plate and fixed a place for him at the table. She was full of chatter, and she was happy, and he let her ramble on through the meal, and afterward he insisted on helping her with the dishes.

Then they sat on the skimpy porch, and the air was full of summer flavor, the scent of flowers and dust and grass. "Papa and the others ought to be two-thirds there by now," Emily said. "It's hard to wait, Ben. Waiting's lonesome." She laced her arm through his and put her head against his shoulder. "And you've been gone a long time. Forever, it seemed."

"Oh, it wasn't that long. There have been some changes around here. I stopped at one of the farms. Saw some others. Dan Canby's name was mentioned."

"Sure, he's behind it all. Loans and giving them a discount at his store. He never gave anyone else a discount, Ben."

"Amy Leland ever get any more coaches?"

"The major found her three, but that's all. I heard talk that Canby wanted to buy her out, but she wouldn't sell. I know she turned him down when he offered her a loan so she could buy coaches." She turned her head and looked at him. "Ben, if anyone besides you had burned her out, I don't think she would have taken it. I think she'd have gone to Canby and fought with him. I'm sure she loves you, Ben."

He laughed. "You're having smoke dreams, Emily. Why, there's never been—"

"There doesn't have to be," she said. "Ben, a woman knows. She won't even speak to me, and that's because of you. Because you took me home and kept me at the post after the fire. I know what the talk is."

"Just what is it?"

She shook her head. "Ask Dan Canby."

"Why, I'll surely do that," he said, rising.

She took his arm to pull him back. "You're not leaving now?"

"I figured to ride on tonight, Emily."

"Ben, you don't have to do that. You can stay here."

He shook his head. "That might not sound so good if it was mentioned." Then he pulled her to her feet and put his arms around her. "I'll be around awhile now. I'll be back." He kissed her, not gently; he wanted her to know the hungers he had. Then he released her and went to his horse.

When he arrived in town, it was late, and the only lamps burning were in Blaine's building, and he wondered who occupied it now. The answer came to him when a colored police sergeant stepped out into the street and pointed a pistol at him. "Halt there," the sergeant said. "It way aftah curfew. Come in de light."

Talon eased his horse over, and the sergeant saw the uniform, and he grinned and put his pistol away. "Ah didn't recognize you, saagint. Would you care to step inside, suh?"

It was a question, and technically a choice, only Talon knew that it wasn't. He tied his horse and stepped inside; the place had been turned into a police barracks, with cells and squad room in back and Blaine's office now occupied by a pink-cheeked lieutenant who resented being wakened.

He rubbed his eyes and looked at Ben Talon and said, "Don't you know you can get shot for being out after curfew, sergeant?"

"I didn't know there was a curfew, sir. There's never been a need for one."

"My decision on that," the officer said. "You're Sergeant Talon, I take it. Been south with some sort of detached duty. I'm Lieutenant Ballard. For your information, sergeant, no one is allowed on the streets after ten o'clock. At sunrise the curfew is lifted."

"Why?"

"Because it's daylight, of course!"

"I meant, sir, why have a curfew at all? Has there been any trouble in town?"

"No, but Mr. Canby thought that a police barracks here would discourage any prospect of it," Ballard said. He was young, in his middle twenties, a man with no military experience and, Talon guessed, much less training. These commissions were political appointments, and although Ballard wore an Army uniform, his rank was only a token and he had no genuine status among military men. He knew it, and he was stiff with resentment.

Ben Talon said gently, "Well, now, I'll tell you something. Dan Canby is getting too damned big for his own britches.

Can't you see the man's out to feather his own nest?" He sat on the edge of the lieutenant's desk and ticked the points off on his fingers. "First, we have Canby picking out land for the farmers and catering to them through the bank and the store. Now suppose these men don't make it. Not all of them, but some of them. So what happens to the land when it goes bust? Canby has a lien on it. Can you see what's coming next? He's got a toehold, and he'll push until he's backed Vale or anyone else into the corner. Hell, he has the money to do it."

"These farmers have rights, Talon."

"Certainly. But is it really their rights Canby wants you to protect?" He shook his head. "Think about it and you'll see that it isn't. Lieutenant, you seem like a nice fella. Do yourself a favor and think about this before you throw all the force at your command on Dan Canby's side."

"Is there something personal between you and this Canby, sergeant?"

"No, I like him. And you might say that we're friends. But I can see what's happening, and I don't like it. Just look carefully before you jump, will you?"

Ballard gnawed his lip. "I should be offended, but somehow I'm not, sergeant. In time I may even thank you for the advice." He smiled and offered his hand. "Good night. Come and go as you please—I'll tell my men."

10

AMY LELAND was sitting in Major Harry Bolton's quarters by invitation. Ben Talon was there, and the orderly was clearing the table and setting out the coffee; he asked the major if there was anything else, and there wasn't, so he left.

Bolton settled in an easy chair and crossed his legs. "Miss Leland, as military governor of this sector, I have a great deal of power, and because of that, I must be very careful to exercise it wisely. It just wouldn't do, you see, to place restrictions on this and that and hope for the best; the police do that, and it doesn't get them very far. Every time they run up against something they don't like, they pass a law against it. So in the year I've been here, I may seem to have done nothing in particular for the welfare of Texas. I believe I have accomplished a great deal because in that year I am sure I have isolated one of the major handicaps you have to recovery." He glanced at Talon, then at Amy Leland. "Your partner, Dan Canby. This man can and will, in the space of another year, strip this country and put the profit in his pocket."

He put it out to her as though he expected her to argue, to disagree, and he was mildly surprised when she nodded and said, "Yes, I have to agree with you, major. For a long time I thought Dan was a sharp man who wanted to do very well in business. But it's more than that. He wants to do everything his way and wants everyone to do it his way, and he just can't settle for any less than that."

Bolton said, "I believe my primary function is to stop

Canby from gaining further control. I'm not after the man. I don't want to deprive him of his enterprises, but I believe that Canby would encourage trouble to the point of one man shooting another if he could profit by it. This was demonstrated to me when we burned the coaches."

"He was sore and lost his head," Ben Talon put in.

"Ben, this habit of yours of giving the other man the benefit of the doubt may do you in one of these days," Bolton said. "No, Dan Canby wasn't displaying his temper. He was displaying a greed that I find dangerous." He brought out a cigar and licked it before putting a match to it. "I've been thinking about this for a long time, and I think I have something, but it will require your cooperation."

"Major, I'll do what I have to do. You've been more than fair with me. If nothing more, it'll be a favor repaid."

"Fine," Bolton said. "As a military man I'd like to say that one way to defeat the enemy is to spread him thin, and generally this is accomplished by stretching his supply lines. Dan Canby needs your wagons, Miss Leland. Perhaps he was thinking of that when you and he became partners. It's a certainty that he'd have difficulty stocking his store if he didn't have a way to haul goods from Galveston. There are two ways to put a crimp in him. One is to sell out to him; this would require a large amount of cash. The second is to refuse to haul for him, thereby causing him to split the company, take half the wagons and men, and—"

"He doesn't have half the wagons," she said. "And I don't have half of his store. He has a third interest in the freight line, and I have a third interest in the store."

"Suppose he offered to buy you out," Talon said. "How much are you worth, Amy?"

She considered it. "Twenty-five thousand. With the three coaches running we still have the mail to carry and the way open to build up again. Yes, twenty-five thousand would be a very reasonable price."

Ben Talon raised an eyebrow. "That ought to hit his cash pretty hard."

"I don't think he'd buy," Amy maintained. "Dan wouldn't be fool enough to strap himself like that."

"Yes, I rather thought it would be like that," Bolton said.

"I've prepared an order for you, Miss Leland. With the Texas Rangers being reactivated under military assistance, I'll need every wagon you have available to haul on Army contract. The Comanches are beginning to cause a bit of a stir around Fredericksburg, and we think it advisable to erect a series of posts with the quickest dispatch." He smiled around his cigar. "This will keep you from losing money and at the same time force Dan Canby to spend a lot of money going into the freighting business, or close his store. It will also save you the trouble of fighting this out with Canby; he'll have to come to me with his complaint."

"Oh, he will," Amy said. "You can bet on it."

Bolton frowned and pulled at his mustache. "I don't like what Canby is doing with these farmers. The cattlemen are gone, and those who have been left behind won't do anything until the owners get back. And when they do, these farmers will think all hell broke loose."

Ben Talon said, "Care for an opinion, sir?"

"Sure."

"The farmers are here to stay."

They looked at him a moment, then Amy Leland laughed. "Ben, that's ridiculous. This has always been open range."

"It won't stay that way," he said. "It'll change. We all change every day, a little bit, and maybe we don't notice it until one day we look into a mirror and find that we're old." He shook his head. "I've been thinking about it, major, and I've made up my mind. The farmers will stay. Not all of them, but some will, and more will come. The Indians saw this happening, wagon after wagon, and they killed off some and more came. It's the same here now. Vale and Early and the others, they'll just have to learn to accept it. The land *is* open range, and any of it can be homesteaded."

The reasoning was not lost on Bolton or on Amy Leland; they sat quietly for several minutes, then Amy said, "Ben, instead of getting the farmers out, you'd rather work to keep them and the cattlemen from fighting. Is that it?"

"Well, in a roundabout way, Amy. The way I see it, Dan Canby wants them to fight. He wants to see men riding with rifle and torch. Eventually the farmer has to give in or get killed, and he pulls out. Then Canby forecloses on the place and either sells it again to another farmer or hangs onto it as a wedge to split up the range."

"Now I just don't believe he's going to do that," Amy said quickly. "You're both forgetting one thing: Dan's a Texan. He wouldn't—'

"He would," Ben Talon said so definitely that she closed her mouth and argued no further.

Later he drove her to town in a military ambulance and helped her down. She started to go in, then stopped and said, "Ben, I feel that we're no longer on the same side anymore, and it bothers me."

"We can't always agree, Amy."

She leaned against her door and crossed her arms. "I didn't think it was going to be like this when the war was over. Win or lose, I believed it would be different."

"What did you think it would be like?"

"Oh, people coming back and working, as they always did, with everybody pretty much the same. I just didn't think that while men were gone, others, myself included, would be —gathering together all the good things so that there wasn't anything left."

"War or no war, opportunities went on," Talon said. "You took them as they came along. It's not bad to take, Amy. It's bad when you hug a thing so tight it chokes."

"And that's what Dan's doing?"

"You know he is. You know the first thing on Dan's mind has always been money—money to use, money to build with, money to expand and build more with. Not just money for its own sake, on any terms whatever. In his own way he's a realist, and he's taken care of Dan Canby, and he's helped this country to make a recovery in the process. The same way you have. But somewhere Dan's gone over the edge. Maybe it happened when the wagons were burned, but I think it started long before that. But he's going to be stopped, and stopped hard. He'll need a lot of help when it happens, Amy." He touched the beak of his forager cap. "Good night."

She reached out and touched his arm. "Ben, are you and Emily Vale going to get married?"

"We've never spoke of it."

"Are you going to tell me it's none of my business?"

He shook his head. "Not you, Amy. Someone else maybe, but not you. We've been friends, haven't we?"

"Good night," she said and quickly turned and went inside.

He waited a moment, then mounted the rig and drove back to the post.

Dan Canby stormed and fumed and swore at Major Bolton, and none of it did him any good; the major assured him that he had a right to commandeer anything he needed, and that included banks and stores, in case Canby wanted to make trouble, and if that wasn't enough, he could move the troops into town and Canby could conduct his business with a lieutenant looking over his shoulder.

Canby left the post, still yelling about damned Yankees, but he had to look elsewhere for wagons.

Fred Early was the first to return home; it was in September, and Jonas Vale and what remained of the hands rode in a week later. Border bandits, Indians, stampedes, and trouble in Kansas had wiped more than twenty men off the payroll, and George Vale had never reached Ellsworth. A storm had stampeded the cattle, and he'd been unlucky. They found his watch and part of his slicker and his pistol some distance away, but nothing more.

Jonas Vale sent word around the country that he was paying off, and the families of the dead men came and stood in line with the cowboys, and Jonas paid the families a full share. Some of the men had no families, and Jonas split this money and gave it to the women who had no men now.

Ben Talon was there when Jonas Vale paid off, and afterward there was a barbecue in the yard, and it was dark before everyone had left. Jonas Vale watched them leave, said good-bye to them, then walked around the empty yard as though he wished they hadn't gone and left him with all this. He was an older man now, a hard-used man; the responsibility of all of this was his.

Ben Talon sat on the step smoking a cigar, and finally Jonas came over and sat down. "You don't know how often I thought of home," Jonas said. "Man, it gets to be an ache inside you after a while." He glanced at Talon and smiled. "You've done a lot for the Vales. I guess you've got your reasons."

"I've always steered clear of men who did things without reasons."

"Yeah, even a bad one's better than none," Jonas said. "Funny thing, though, when Pa was alive, I'd as soon go off half-cocked as not. But when he died, it all changed. After the stampede, when he was found—or what we could find—the fellas gathered around and just looked at the ground; then they looked at me, and I just couldn't make any more mistakes, Ben. Every decision I made had to be a good one. I guess that's the reason I'm not having my horse saddled to ride on the farmers tonight."

"Expect you saw a couple of their places on the way in."

"Yeah, and the wranglers told me as soon as I dismounted. Is it Canby's doing?"

"I think it is. It's an opinion that's not completely popular." He brought out two cigars and offered one to Jonas. "You're a rich man now, Jonas. You can put on men, pay regular wages, and make next year's drive from your front porch, with a hired trail boss doing the hard work. But as I see it, you and Early can pull power away from Canby because you have money."

"Well, I sure as hell won't be using his bank," Jonas Vale said. "I've got to settle with Amy Leland, pay my bill at Canby's, and then I'm clear with the world."

"A man can't ask for much more, can he?" Ben got up and stretched. "Guess I'll say good night to Emily and ride back. Tomorrow I'm supposed to go to Wichita Falls for a month."

"Ben, am I going to have you for a brother-in-law?"

"Why? Does the idea bother you?"

"No. I just wondered if it bothered you."

"What made you stop fighting the war?" Talon asked.

"I don't know. Somewhere between here and Kansas I got it through my head that it was over. And I've stopped being ashamed because we lost it."

Dan Canby shot Jonas Vale on a Saturday afternoon. The argument started over two barrels of flour; Vale insisted that he had taken three barrels, and Canby stood pat that he had loaded five in the wagons, and the upshot of it was that

Canby called Vale a damned liar and a cheapskate who was trying to weasel out of paying his bill in full.

There was no argument that Jonas Vale reached for his gun first; he fired first, the bullet missing Canby by a bare fraction, then Canby shot him through the body, and Jonas Vale staggered out of the store and into the street.

Vale was still alive when several men hurriedly carried him to the doctor's office, but it didn't look as though he'd last long.

Before the police could arrest Dan Canby, he got on his horse and rode out to the post and turned himself over to Major Bolton, who held him until two of his officers could conduct a complete investigation.

Lieutenant Ballard of the police force had already rounded up witnesses—the two clerks in the store and some onlookers on the street who had seen the tag end of it—and when Bolton was finished, he released Canby, having nothing to hold him on or charge him with.

Ben Talon was up on the Sweetwater with a company of engineers, building Fort Elliott, when a courier coming north with dispatches brought him the news, along with an order from Major Bolton to return as soon as possible.

It was almost four days before Ben Talon returned on a jaded horse; he turned it over to one of the stable detail and went immediately to Bolton's office and was told that he was in town. Catching up a fresh horse, Talon rode into town, and as he approached Amy Leland's stable yard, he saw Bolton's horse tied outside. He stopped, tied up, and went in.

Amy was cleaning out her desk, packing everything into wooden boxes. She looked up, saw him, and said, "Hello, stranger."

Bolton turned around, shook Talon's hand, then said, "Canby bought her out. Cash on the barrel head."

"Your price, Amy?"

"Yes, twenty-five thousand." She sat down on one of the boxes and folded her hands. "I was wrong, Ben. He wants it all."

"Canby wants to negotiate a new contract with the Army," Bolton said. "I may have to move troops in, but I don't want to do that, and Canby knows it." He blew out a long breath.

"Emily Vale wants to see you, Ben. Jonas has made it, but he's going to be a very sick man for quite a while. And there's talk around town that the farmers will take Vales' place over. I even suspect that Fred Early is eying that range. It's for the grabbing, you know." He glanced briefly at Amy Leland. "Ben, I can arrange a discharge for you any time if you want it. But we can't have any shooting or the start of anything like that. If factions get to potting at one another, I don't think there are enough troops in Texas to stop it."

"I'll ride out there," Talon said. "What are you going to do now, Amy?"

"Fight," she said. "Dan Canby has overlooked one thing: I'm a woman, and he couldn't shoot me in an argument. And he's given me a weapon. Twenty-five thousand dollars."

"Compared to what Dan is worth—"

"I know, but I think it's enough. Ben, you tell Emily how sorry we've all been about Jonas and all this trouble."

"All right," he said and went out to his horse.

He pushed on the ride south, fast march, dismounting at regular intervals to rest the horse, then swinging up and riding fast. By midafternoon he reached the Vale place and swung down near the well, tying up there. A dozen men loafed near the corral, talking and smoking. Talon was not a rancher, but he knew that there was little idleness on a ranch that made money.

Emily came out and started toward him, but he waved her back, and she stopped by the porch, not understanding this. Talon unbuckled his pistol belt and hung it over the saddle, then walked across the yard to where the men stood.

"Who's the foreman around here?" he asked.

One man took his time, saying finally, "He quit. Day before yesterday."

"Don't you men have anything to do?"

They looked at each other, then one man eased out in front. "I guess we do, but no one's give us any orders." He nodded toward Emily Vale standing across the yard. "She told us to do somethin', but she don't really know what it's all about."

"Try to remember what it was," Talon suggested.

"Can't," the man said.

He grinned just a split instant before Talon hit him, slamming him back into his friends with enough force to bowl two over and send the man back against the corral post. Blood ran from the man's face, and he slowly, carefully pushed himself erect.

"Remember now?" Talon asked.

"I remember less," the man said, and because he was Texan and not afraid of anything, he made his rush, arms flailing unskillfully. Talon met him, weathered a rain of fists, then grappled with the man. He locked his head in the crook of his arm and brought his hard cavalryman's boots down on the cowboy's toes and repeatedly hit him in the face, bloodying his nose and cutting him about the eyes.

Then he spun him away, caught him by the front of the vest, and sledgehammered him on the jaw. The man turned into a rag and fell, and Talon dragged him to the horse trough and dumped him in, ducking him twice before he hauled him out.

He propped the man up against the corral and shook him until his eyes focused. "Can you hear me? My name is SIR, and when I speak, you jump. I'll give orders around here, and I want to see head down and ass up. UNDERSTAND!"

The man nodded, and Talon let him go; he would have fallen again if two friends hadn't rushed in to support him. He looked at each of them. "Do I have to repeat myself with any of you? If I do, just step up and start swinging."

They looked around, exchanged glances, then another man shifted his tobacco and said, "I guess we heah you cleah, sur. An' ah remember what it was we was to do."

If they expected him to move, they guessed wrong; he stood there, and they left, moving as if they had someplace to go now, and when they'd caught up their horses and ridden out, he walked over to the porch.

Emily came to him; he folded his arms around her, and she began to cry, and he let it go this way for several minutes; then with his arm around her he took her into the house. She needed something to do, so he told her to fix him something to eat, and this calmed her, let her focus on something besides trouble.

He said, "I'm staying, Emily."

For a moment she seemed not to hear him; then she turned around and looked at him, not saying anything; she seemed almost afraid to speak.

"For good, Emily. Major Bolton said I could have my discharge. Will you marry me, Emily?"

"Ben—"

"I love you, Emily. I guess from the first time in Canby's store I knew there wasn't going to be anyone else. You knew it, too, didn't you?"

"Yes, Ben."

"I was a fool to wait this long. Hadn't intended to. Jonas asked me before I rode north if I was going to be his brother-in-law. He seemed to like the idea." He got up and came around the table and put his arms around her. "You don't have to answer now if you want to think about it."

"I don't have to think about it," she said softly. "I want to marry you, Ben. Whenever you want."

"Soon," he said. "We'll go to town tomorrow."

A wagon came into the yard, and he stepped back, looked out the kitchen window, then stepped outside. The wagon stopped near the porch. A heavy man in overalls sat on the seat; he had two strapping boys with him.

"Howdy there," the man said. "Name's Miller. My boys." He looked around. "This the Vale place? It don't look like much. Have a fire? Bad, fires." He finally got around to studying Ben Talon, then Emily stepped out and stood by Ben, her hand lightly on his arm. "Hear in town that this place is on the die-up."

"You heard wrong," Ben Talon said.

The man turned this over in his head, then said, "I got the banker's say-so on it. Likely he'd know." He looked around again. "Crossed a creek a mile back. Figure I'll build there, near the road."

"My advice is not to, because if you do, we'll move you out." Ben Talon pointed. "There's land to the south, some farmers living there. Go there if you want, but stay away from that creek."

"I like to make up my own mind," Miller said. "The land looks good, and it suits me. My boys and I will each take a section."

It was an alarming thing to hear, and Talon suddenly understood what made cattlemen grab their rifles and start shooting. But he kept his voice down and his temper in place. "Mr. Miller, this ranch is not going to fight with the farmers. There's a place for each of us. If you want a section, take it to the south. There's water there and your kind of people. But don't cut up this ranch to suit your fancy. And not three sections. You'll have trouble, and I don't think you can handle it."

"The land's free."

"Yes, it is, but not free to make a hog of yourself."

"That's kind of insulting," Miller said. "Wouldn't you say so, Milo, Kyle?"

"It did sound that way," the older son said. He kept looking at Emily and smiling. "You belong to anybody, or are you free, too?"

Ben Talon turned, took one long step, picked up the Spencer repeater resting just inside the door, levered one into the chamber, and pointed it at the father. "Now turn your wagon south, friend. I won't bother to tell you again."

"The land's free," Miller said, lifting the reins. "You're only one man. We can fight, too."

"I don't want to fight, you damned fool! Are you so blind you can't see that?" He waved the muzzle of the gun. "Go on, you've overstayed your welcome."

They drove out and did not turn south; he had not expected Miller to, for the man was a mule bent on having his own way. Talon feared him, feared the relentless stubbornness in the man, for Miller was the very kind that would have to be pushed off, the very kind that would start what none of them really wanted started.

11

IN DAN CANBY'S MIND, the brightest day came in late February when Maj. Harry Bolton got his orders; the Army was pulling out, ending the governmental duties, and uniting to put down the Comanche trouble, which was growing more dangerous each day.

The police would be withdrawn from counties that went ahead with elections and created an office of sheriff to maintain law and order; it was the very thing Canby wanted, and he immediately had a stack of posters printed, announcing Pete Field as candidate. Field hadn't been doing much since the hide business collapsed; he worked for Canby, doing as he was told, and ran his blacksmith business when he felt like it or the work piled up.

Dan Canby felt that he was the best choice for sheriff.

Amy Leland did not.

As soon as she heard about it, she rented a buggy and drove south to the Vale place. Jonas Vale, partially recovered, had been sent East for further treatment. Meantime Ben had spent the winter rebuilding the house; it stood on the old site, broad and rambling, with a porch running around all four sides. When she stopped in the yard, a man came from the barn and took the rig, and Emily came out of the house.

Talon was out and wouldn't return until evening, but Emily insisted that Amy come inside and wait; she could spend the night and return to town in the morning.

It was almost dark when Talon returned with a crew of twenty men. He paused on the porch to remove his spurs and chaps and pistol belt, then stepped into the warm kitchen.

Emily was fixing supper, and Amy was helping her, and Talon smiled, surprised, but pleased. "Well, Amy, I haven't seen you all winter. What have you been doing with yourself?"

"Sitting on my money and watching Dan Canby grow," she said. "Ben, did you know that the Army has pulled out?"

He shook his head. "I've been on the range for nearly six weeks now. We're rounding up for another drive in a month."

"Pete Field is running for sheriff. Canby's candidate." She showed him one of the posters that were being put up everywhere.

He read it and laughed. "Honest? Hard-working? People's choice?" He threw it down. "Why doesn't Canby run himself? Pete's been a solid Canby man since he got a taste of easy money."

"He can't run unopposed," Amy Leland said, then explained the conditions of police withdrawal. "Of course, Canby will pay some fool to run against Field, someone who's bound to lose. I'm not going to sit by and see that happen, Ben."

"Get a good man who can beat Field."

"That's why I came to see you."

He looked at her, then shook his head. "You don't want me to run. Oh, no, I've got enough to do. Sodbusters moving in on us, putting up fences, and cattle to get to market. Amy, you're out of your mind."

"Ben, people know you. They trust you. I think you'd get a large share of the farmers' vote, too, because you've been fair to them. Ben, I want you to think about it."

"There's nothing to think about," he said. "I don't want it. Get someone else."

"Ben, there isn't anyone else."

"That's ridiculous. Are you telling me there isn't one man in this whole county who's better than Pete Field?" He sat down and kept shaking his head. "Amy, I'm thirty-four years old, and I've got a wife who's going to have a baby in another six months. I've got cattle to get to market in Kansas, and farmers trying to cut up our land and just looking for an excuse to take a shot at our riders. Now I just don't need the added responsibility of being sheriff. So forget it."

"Is that your final word, Ben?"

"It has to be." He leaned forward and braced his forearms

on the table top. "Amy, I'm just like any other man, willing to coast along until he's pushed into doing something to take care of himself. We don't fence range because no one is chipping at our boundary, and George Vale never put a brand on a steer until the hide hunters started stripping the range; an earmark had always been enough between friends. But the hide hunters were going blind, it seemed, so he had to hotiron a slash across the flank. One of these days I'll probably have to paint 'em blue because we've already lost a few head to the farmers who just can't understand how an animal that isn't tied or fenced can be someone's property. And I figured the only way to stop these farmers from cutting Vale land to pieces was to legally own the land, so this winter sixty riders have filed on a section apiece with the land office in Austin; they've built cabins and are batching it or have moved their families in. When they prove up on it, Jonas and I will buy the land from them, and then we'll divide it between us. There isn't any more land on this range to be had." He shook his head. "No, I'm not going to run for sheriff or anything else."

"Ben, someone has to do something."

"You do it."

She looked at him oddly. "Me?"

"Why not? You ought to do something for yourself. The Army set you up in business with mules and stages. You're still a partner in Canby's store, and, like it or not, he has to give you a cut of the profits. You do something." He leaned forward and tapped her on the arm. "But understand something, Amy—this brand is not afraid of Dan Canby. I have the men and the money to fight him, and if he starts to squeeze me, we'll just have to take him apart to protect ourselves. We're not going to hog land or drive the farmers out; the ones who are here can stay. But we'll take care of ourselves."

"Ben, this isn't like you."

"What is it like? I have new responsibilities now, and I'll take care of them. If you want to stop Canby from grabbing it all, then you do it."

"How?"

"Think of something. You're not stupid. How much is it worth to you?"

"What do you mean?"

"I mean, is it worth enough for you to risk your money on? You don't have any hesitation in asking someone else to put everything on the block." He leaned back in his chair and studied her.

"Ben, it's easy for you to say, but there are limits to what a woman can do." She looked at Emily. "You're not helping me much."

"You always gave me the impression that you could take care of yourself. So go ahead."

"That's an easy way to push it off onto someone else."

"Amy, I'm not pushing anything," Talon said. "I'm just telling you as plain as I can that I have plenty of trouble of my own. Hell, just last week the Comanches cut right across my place to the north of here. It scared the devil out of Miller and his family."

She frowned a moment. "Is he the one who moved in on your creek?" He nodded. "I heard you threatened to run him off, give him a place to the south. But he called your bluff and moved in anyway."

"Miller is my business," Talon told her. "It's going to stay that way. And in case Dan Canby asks my intentions, tell him I leave people alone and like to be left alone. Don't send any more farmers out here."

She sighed and got up. "I wish you'd change your mind, Ben."

"Can't," he said. "It isn't that I don't want to—it's just that this is my most urgent responsibility."

"But sometimes a man takes on more because he has to."

"Not this man," he said, and that ended it.

Dan Canby liked to spend his idle hours thinking of all the money he was going to make if the Army cleaned up the Indian trouble and if the cattlemen let the farmers alone so they could bring in crops and pay back all the money they had borrowed from him. This was, Canby knew, the biggest gamble he had ever taken; he was spread so thin that it hurt to think about it, but he kept telling himself that if he hadn't grabbed when he had the chance, Yankees would have snatched at the opportunity.

He firmly believed that it was the Canby nerve and Canby money that kept them out of the county. He knew what was going on in Texas, the Yankee money pouring in and Yankees moving in along with it to run things to suit themselves and putting ninety cents of every dollar into their own pockets.

There were times when he wished he hadn't bought the freight line; it was paying its own way, even making a little money, but he needed stages running on regular schedules to show the kind of profit he liked. Yet he just didn't have the capital now to build it up again, and there was no chance at all of getting Army equipment.

Canby's office in the bank was the mecca of all his business activities; when a man wanted credit at the store, or something hauled, or a loan, he came to the office, passed through a clerk who screened him, and then Canby made his judgments.

Amos Miller sprawled in his chair; he seemed incapable of sitting upright. He was a rough-mannered man with an eternal sulk on his face. "Simple," he said. "I need more money. Some of my seed spoiled."

There was manure on his boots and dirt under his fingernails, and he kept spitting tobacco, missing the spittoon half the time. Dan Canby looked at the records a moment. "Miller, I've loaned you seven hundred in cash, and you've run up a three-hundred-dollar bill at the store. You owe others in town."

"A man has to live. You told me I could get a start here. Told me you'd back me."

"Are you going to get a crop in this year, Miller?"

"Some. What do you expect of a man in his first year? He's got to get settled, don't he?" He shifted in his chair and scraped the soles of his boots together, dropping pieces of dried manure on Canby's floor. Then he made small sweeping motions with his feet, pushing the pieces away from him. "I don't trust them cowboys. That Talon fella, either. Indians passed my place awhile back. A man's got to take care of himself first, then worry about plantin'." He scratched his unshaven cheek and smiled. "I figure you'll loan me the money, Mr. Canby. If I don't get it, I'll pull up stakes. Done it before. Do it again if I have to."

"Is that the kind of responsibility you feel toward people who've helped you?" Canby asked.

"Said a man's got to take care of himself first, didn't I?"

Dan Canby studied him a moment, then got up and opened his office door. He spoke to a clerk. "Adam, will you open the front door and hold it open?"

"Certainly, Mr. Canby."

Turning back to Amos Miller, Canby pounced on him, grabbed him by the shirt front, and jerked him out of the chair. Miller, surprised by this violence, offered no resistance for a moment, but the handling bumped his vast pride and his temper took control. He bellowed like a gored bull, struck Canby a mighty but clumsy blow that lifted Canby clean over the desk, and deposited him on the floor.

His swivel chair upset and kited into the corner, the back broken cleanly off, and then Canby scrambled to his feet and charged Amos Miller, weathering a flurry of wild swings in order to get into the man. He flailed Miller in the face, stomped on his toes, hit him in the stomach, and propelled him backward to escape this punishment.

They passed through the door of Canby's office, and Miller, to halt the retreat, grabbed the door frame with both hands and left himself wide open. Canby laid a sledgehammer fist against the farmer's face, bringing blood and cutting him to the bone, and the blow broke Miller's grip, sailed him flat on his back into the main room of the bank.

Customers gawked, and Canby grabbed Miller, dragged him to the front door, and pitched him headfirst into the street. The farmer tried to get up, but his strength was gone, and he rolled over and looked at Canby.

"You want to pull stakes, Miller? Then, by God, you pull 'em and be quick about it. Day after tomorrow I'll be riding to your place, and if you're not gone, you'll sure as hell wish you were." He turned back inside the bank, speaking to the clerk. "Close the door, Adam; we're letting flies in."

A quickly gathered crowd watched Miller get to his feet and paw at the blood on his face. He looked around and said, "Somebody give me a gun."

"Now you don't want to do that, mister," a man said. "Why don't you go home?"

Miller thought of an angry reply to this but realized that he'd made a fool of himself, and his only desire was to get away from them.

His wagon was down the street; he went to it, climbed aboard, and drove slowly out of town. His head was beginning to ache badly, and each jolt of the wagon sent pain around his skull to settle behind his eyes. His lips, puffed now so that he could not close them naturally, had stopped bleeding, and a large swelling began under his left eye. By the time he reached his own place, the eye was closed completely.

His sons were full of questions when they helped him down, and he grew angry at them and cuffed them and went into the house, where his wife made him go to bed. She got a pan of water and bathed his face and kept up a running chirp of sympathy, while his daughters hung back, waiting to see which way his temper would swing.

"Let Canby come to me," he said. "I'll kill him!"

His wife didn't ask if he'd gotten the money; she knew that he hadn't and that somehow it had led to this. She did what she could for him, then left him alone.

The boys stayed close to the house, for they had learned that he was an unpredictable man in defeat, and when his temper was up, they could expect the worst.

Milo, the older one, saw Indians in the late afternoon and told his brother. Together they went into the house to tell their mother, but since their father was sleeping and hated to be disturbed, they decided to say nothing and handle it themselves.

The two boys, armed with shotguns, went outside and saw nearly a hundred Indians topping a slight rise a half mile from the creek; they sat their ponies and watched, then they broke and came down off the hill, running, yelling. The boys stupidly fired their shotguns, although the range was still too long for a good rifle.

Kyle managed to reload his shotgun as the Indians reached the yard. Amos Miller, startled by the noise, bowled out of the door just as Kyle fired again, bringing down an Indian, the only one killed that day. The Indians overran them, and Kyle was driven through with a Comanche lance.

The other boy, starting to run, died with his father by the door. Then the Indians stormed about the yard, destroying everything, while a few dismounted and broke into the house.

Mrs. Miller hit one on the head with a skillet and was promptly killed with a knife. The two girls, locking themselves in a bedroom, were brought out, stripped, and dragged outside and held to the ground while the bravest of the young warriors raped them.

They were not strong girls; they cried and screamed, and finally the Indians grew tired of it, pinned them with lances where they lay, mounted up, and rode off in a southerly direction.

Lt. Joseph Ballard, late commandant of the State Police and now on active duty with the Army, brought a patrol close to the Miller place shortly before sundown, and his scouts reported to him that they had found what remained of the homestead.

Ballard's troop had been nine days in the field now, and the Comanches had led them on a wild chase, always managing to stay ahead of him. They'd run in a wide circle, and he was no nearer to them now than he had been when he'd picked up the trail near the San Saba. He only knew that he was beat and his men were beat and the horses were about through, so he ordered the command to camp the night, build squad fires, set up guards and pickets, and get a burial detail organized.

Ballard walked around while the light lasted and saw everything and wrote it down in a small book for his report, and it was grisly work, especially putting it down about the women. He had the married men take care of them; the bodies were wrapped in blankets and placed in deep graves. It was dark now, and he read the service with the help of a lantern held by the company bugler.

The guards challenged approaching horsemen, then they were let through, and Ben Talon came over and flung off; he had twenty-five men with him, all heavily armed.

"One of my riders saw the fires," Talon said. He had his

look and knew without asking what had happened. He also looked at the soldiers, their dirty clothes and beards, and he knew they had been long on the march.

Ballard was finished; he turned the detail over to the sergeant, and the graves were filled. "One Indian dead," he said, sitting down near a cook fire. "No, we didn't find him, but we found his shield. I understand that a Comanche wouldn't give up his shield while he was alive."

"You're learning," Talon said. "Different from the police, isn't it?"

Ballard smiled and shook his head. "Damn it, I just couldn't catch them!"

"You weren't about to," Talon said. "Any day of the week they can outride you, outfight you, and if you ever do catch them, you'll know it's because they want it and have a trick up their sleeve."

"There was no reason for this attack on this farmer," Ballard said.

"Yes, there was. What started all this, Ballard?"

"Nothing. They just went on the rampage last year."

Ben Talon took off his hat and scratched his head. "We both know better than that. Something happened. Somewhere along the line the Indians figure they've been mistreated. It's enough to set 'em off."

"Well, I don't know." He thought a moment. "Of course, there was that affair around Fredericksburg—some farmers caught an Indian woman and a boy stealing hogs, and before it was over, they'd lost their heads and hung them."

"Now you've got an Indian war."

"Over that? The farmers were tried and sent to prison, Ben."

"That's not enough to satisfy the Comanches," Talon pointed out. "When they speak of justice, they're talking about an eye-for-an-eye sort of thing. Jail, a fine—that's not justice. Just how come they decided to run in this neck of the woods?"

"They were pushed. Colonel Bolton has his troops in the field constantly."

"Colonel?"

"Yes, he got his promotion."

The sergeant came over, saluted, and said, "Burial detail complete, sir. Shall I dismiss the men?"

"Thank you, yes. I want a full guard detail tonight, and pay special watch over the horses. The Comanches may try to raid."

"Not before morning if they do," Talon said.

"I'm just following the book," Ballard said. "You heard the order, sergeant." He waited until the man left before going on. "Ben, I've got an awful lot to learn and not much time in which to learn it. It seems to me that Bolton has a damned small force to put down this kind of trouble. We never have enough men, and we've lost some, too. The Comanches do get tired of running, and the two engagements the Army has had with them didn't turn out well for the Army." He picked up the coffeepot and two cups, filled them, and handed one to Ben Talon. "The farmers have been hit—Miller isn't the only one. His is the fourth place to go. Everyone is raising hell, yelling for the Army to get busy, and the newspapers are printing some nasty stories about military incompetents." He shook his head. "It's getting so that when you take a troop in town people just line the streets to stare and cuss at you."

"The buffalo are going to be thin this year," Ben Talon said. "My men who made the trip north last year told me that hundreds of outfits were cleaning the plains of Kansas of buffalo. I hear there's a camp near the Nations called Adobe Walls."

"Who gives a God-damn about the buffalo?"

"If I was you, I'd care a lot, Joe. The Comanches live off the buffalo. So do the Arapaho and Kiowa. When the buffalo stop migrating and the Indians start to starve and freeze, you'll see a war from one end of Texas clear to the Canadian border. They can't live without the buffalo, and they'll do their damnedest to take two white men with every one of them that dies." He stood up and quickly drank the rest of his coffee. "I'm going back to my place. Likely there won't be trouble."

"I wouldn't count on it."

"Well, I do," Ben Talon said, "and I'll tell you why. We've got men and they're armed. They're full of Indian savvy. The

Comanches know what it'll cost to raid a Texas ranch. We'd fight on their terms, and they don't want that. Joe, remember this: they're trying to kill as many of us as they can and lose as few as they can in doing it. You come up with an idea that'll change that around, and the Comanches won't be long in suing for peace."

12

THAT SPRING eleven major herds were driven north to market, with the Early-Vale brand sixth largest. They followed old trails to new towns: Wichita, Abilene, and a place at the end of track called Dodge City. They left Texas, cattle and men and horses, and Texas would not see them again for eight and a half months, and she would never see some of these men again, for the news was common that the Comanche and the Kiowa and the Arapaho were united now for the big war to drive the white man out and bring the buffalo back.

There had been much singing and dancing and making of medicine.

And there was constant raiding.

Before the heat of summer came, Indians had leveled a dozen small ranches, killed half a hundred men, and had taken more than ten girls as prisoners.

They struck in the vicinity of Fredericksburg, ran north to Sherman, ducked up into the Indian Nations for a breather, then moved southwest as far as Coleman, burning, killing, while the Army ran after them and couldn't stop them.

Most of the time they couldn't even catch them.

It had all started as Texas business, but it didn't stay that way for long. Eastern newspapers began to pick up the story, and when it grew big enough, they sent a flood of reporters and correspondents to cover the news.

The farmers, who had come to Texas in response to the promotion of land speculators, were the primary target of the Indians. It was farmers who plowed under the grass, and this drove the Indians to a fury.

To Dan Canby's way of thinking, this could ruin him. The Indians and the Texas cattlemen didn't get along, but they didn't fight all the time, and since he had put his money into backing the farmers, trouble to them was deep trouble for him.

Many of them were packing up, leaving.

Many had already gone, leaving dead unburied and the place a burned ruin.

And more than a few never lived long enough to leave.

Which left Dan Canby sitting in his bank, holding a lot of paper on land that he couldn't readily sell.

Heavily armed and mounted on a fast horse, he rode alone to Fort Griffin to see Colonel Bolton about getting the Army to increase their patrol activity.

Bolton assured him that this was impossible; the Army was spread much too thin now. The meeting began to strain their tempers, so that in the end nothing was accomplished and a lot of harsh words had been passed back and forth.

Dan Canby returned to Abilene. He arrived late in the evening, but went to the hotel in spite of that and knocked on Amy Leland's door. He woke her; he could tell by the way she spoke, and he identified himself, and she opened the door for him.

He paused in the hall long enough to beat dust from his clothes, then stepped inside while she adjusted the table lamp. "Dan, it's after eleven o'clock."

"Yes, yes," he said impatiently. "I've been to see that fool Bolton. He says he can't send a company here."

"Well, you really didn't expect him to, did you?" She belted her robe and sat down in a deep chair. "What do you want, Dan?"

He lit a cigar and rolled it from one side of his mouth to the other. "I've made up my mind that if the Army can't stop this Indian trouble, then it's up to me."

"You're going out and fight them all by yourself. How brave."

"Don't be funny," he suggested. "Amy, I want to recruit a private army, say two hundred men. That's all I'll need, two hundred men and thirty days. After that, there won't be any more Indian trouble."

"I don't think the Army will let you do that, Dan."

"How can they stop me? By the time they find me, I'll have solved their problems for them. Hell, Amy, it takes a Texan to fight Indians. Not these Yankee cavalrymen with their pack horses and sabers." He rubbed his hands together. "I figure I can get the men. Pay them one hundred dollars."

She did some mental arithmetic. "Twenty thousand dollars?"

He nodded. "You'd have to loan it to me, Amy. I just don't have that kind of cash now."

For a moment she studied him carefully, then said, "Dan, is there anything—anything at all that you don't figure you can do better than anyone else?"

"Now that you mention it, no."

"If you do this, you're going to get some good men killed. Maybe yourself, too. If you lose, Dan, you're going to lose it all. Do you understand that? You'll be broke, because the farmers will be gone and you'll be holding a lot of notes you can't collect on, and you'll have to pay back the twenty thousand you want to borrow from me, and I'll take the store in satisfaction of it."

"You wouldn't do that to me, would you, Amy?"

"Yes, if it means cutting you back to size. I liked the old honest, optimistic Dan Canby, but I can't stand the greedy, too-big-for-his-britches Dan Canby. If you want to come downstairs to the hotel safe, I'll get your money. But you'll sign a note for it and put up your store for security."

"That's drawing blood, Amy."

"It's business, the way you've taught it. A deal?"

He laughed. "What choice do I have? I've got to save these farmers to save myself."

The simple way to gather men, Canby knew, was to put on a barbecue and roll out six barrels of beer and a keg of whiskey; he hired three men to ride around the county, passing the word.

The affair was scheduled for Sunday on the courthouse lawn, and the crowd was large, as he'd expected it to be, for social gatherings were few and far between and a person couldn't beat free barbecue and beer.

There were games and sack races and dancing until early evening, and after everyone had eaten, the men gathered on the south side to hear what Canby had to say. They sat on the grass and drank and smoked, and he made his speech, made it carefully, playing on their native prejudice against Indians, and on their fears that what was happening to the farmers could just as easily be happening to them.

Canby was careful not to say anything that these men could really disagree with, and after he had made certain they shared his view that the Army just wasn't doing the job, he gave them his offer: a hundred dollars for one month's work; they would furnish their own horse, gear, gun, and ammunition.

They would, under his command, and the Confederate flag if it made them feel better, wipe out this Indian menace once and for all.

He listened to a lot of opinions. Some liked it, and some didn't, and a lot of men didn't know, but he kept on talking, kept on selling, and when he had sold enough, he began recruiting. He got out a book, and the men formed two lines to sign names or put down their mark, and when this was going well, he turned the recruitment over to one of his bank clerks and came over to where Ben Talon leaned against a tree.

"I didn't see you step up there, Ben," Canby said.

"You're not about to. Dan, this is the dumbest stunt you're ever liable to pull. Leave the Army alone. They'll get the job done."

"Not fast enough."

"You're going to get these men killed."

"They're grown men. They know the risks." He grinned and clamped his teeth firmly into his cigar. "I may surprise you, Ben. The laugh will be on the other end if I do the job and don't get a lot of them killed."

"My opinion stands; this is stupid."

Canby let his pleasure fade. "Ben, some people might say that you're scared."

"You're entitled to an opinion," Talon admitted. "Good luck, Dan." He turned and walked around the stone building and found his wife in the buggy. Amy Leland was there, and they stopped talking when he came up. "Where did Canby get the money to hire men?"

"I loaned it to him," Amy said casually.

"You know, he's apt to get himself killed."

"Yes, I've thought about that, but it's a gamble I'll have to take. Dan doesn't think anyone can lick him, Ben. I think he can be licked. The point is, it can't be a little licking. It's got to be a whopper, something that'll drive him down so hard he'll hurt his knees and have to take the slow way up. It's got to be a licking that will drive sense back into him."

"He stands to lose everything, Amy. Money, his life maybe."

"Yes, I know that. And that's why I want him to do this. He's got to learn that there really is more trouble in this world than he can handle. You won't ride with him?"

"Not a chance," Ben Talon said. "Ready to go home, Emily?"

"Yes, I'm getting tired." She slid over in the seat and he climbed aboard. "Come out if you can, Amy." She adjusted her bonnet, and Talon clucked the team into motion, turning out onto the street.

As soon as Ben Talon reached home, he went into the study and wrote a letter to Col. Harry Bolton and sealed it. He gave it to the horse wrangler and sent him on his way to Fort Griffin, warning him to stay awake and not to loaf along the way.

He didn't like to be the one to tell Bolton about Canby's plan, but someone had to, and Bolton would be sure to hear about it, anyway, and warned this way, he might be able to stop Canby. The Army did not need another force in the field, a force that was ragtag to begin with and possibly at cross purposes with military policy.

The cook went into town with the wagon for supplies and brought back the word that Dan Canby and a hundred men had ridden out the day before, heading northwest toward the Red River, the last known location of the Comanches.

In a sense, Ben Talon was relieved, for he believed that the Comanche bands had already cut back and were running south, regrouping there. If this was correct, then Canby was going to ride his men out, cover a lot of dry Texas real estate and get nothing for his trouble except saddle gall.

What Canby had no way of knowing, and Talon certainly could not know, was that Colonel Bolton and four companies of cavalry had managed to cut the Comanche-Kiowa trail near Palo Duro Creek, just a few miles from the Indian Nations. In a flanking movement Bolton and his force began to run the Indians south, making no contact with them, but keeping them in sight.

The Indians didn't want to fight; they weren't ready because the moon wasn't right and they didn't have the medicine for it, or some other reason; they were in the mood to run, but not too fast, for they wanted to wear the cavalry out, then cut about and kill them.

After four days the Indians stopped at one of Amy Leland's old abandoned relay stations, drank from the well, filled their water bags, and moved on. The cavalry, in close pursuit, did not stop, feeling that their supplies and water would hold out, and they had never before been so close to the enemy.

There was some fighting, sporadic sniping, a delaying action with light casualties on both sides, but the Indians moved on, turning west as though meaning to make a raid on Tascosa, and the Army pursued them, pushing hard to catch them.

For sixteen days the Indians led the Army by the nose, always avoiding contact except for isolated scout activity where a few shots were fired back and forth. Bolton, worn thin by this time, riding a very tired horse, knew that his command could not continue without a rest; he ordered a camp established on the Red River, planning to get on the move again soon enough to keep the Indians running.

But when day came, a thin gray light, the prairie was empty. Each rise was studied carefully through field glasses, and scouts bellied out and had a better look and came back and reported that the Indians were gone.

Dan Canby's citizen army made contact with the Indians on one of the Red's uncharted forks. The Indians were camped when Canby's scouts found them and reported back, and a mood of jubilation swept through the ranks, and Canby was hard put to it to keep them from attacking recklessly right away.

He managed to impose his will on them by threatening not to pay them if they disobeyed his orders, and then he made plans. Splitting the force in three parts, twenty men on each flank and sixty to make the frontal assault, he intended to attack at night. He had already selected several men as lieutenants; they were to be in command of the flanking force and move in when the assault took place.

There was a mass checking and oiling of weapons and a lot of bragging about how many dead Comanches would be left on the prairie come morning.

Canby was careful to keep up an optimistic front, but he knew that he had bought twenty thousand dollars worth of trouble; the scouts had estimated the Indian force at around a hundred and fifty, all fighting men; no squaws or children. Canby's original intention of taking two hundred men had never sounded better, and he was sorry that he had been eager and settled for less. But it was too late to retreat now. A man had to do with what he had, and surprise would help even the odds.

He had them mount up around midnight, and they moved out, splitting into three segments. The night swallowed them, for there was no moon and the stars gave next to no light at all. Yet a man could see, could make out the lay of the land, and Canby moved his men forward with great care; there was no talking or smoking, and the riders tried not to make the saddle leather squeak.

Finally he topped a rise and saw fires in the Indian camp, and this made him pause, for it was a foolish thing to build fires with an army on the prowl, but then he supposed it was like an Indian to do a stupid thing, and thought no more of it.

He led the charge because it was the thing to do, and they went into the camp, shooting and yelling, and a lot of Indians shot back, but it wasn't half as bad as Canby had imagined it would be. He lost a few men, then the flanking force struck with a fury, taking the horse herd in one fell swoop.

Canby led his men through, wheeled, and came back, and

the Indians were a little better organized now, although he supposed that no more than fifty or sixty put up much of a fight.

Some buck put a bullet into Canby's horse and it fell; he pitched off, rolled, and came up shooting, killing a Kiowa who was leveling a rifle at him. Dust was thick now; the horses were milling around, and the air had a dense stench of powder smoke, and bullets were flying about in a fashion he felt most dangerous, so he went belly down on the ground and let the fighting swirl around him.

From his place he could see that the Texans were winning, but it didn't seem that the Comanches were putting up the kind of a fight their reputation called for. Half of them were not fighting at all but crawling around, trying to find someplace to hide.

And the Texans kept riding in and out, shooting at everything that moved, and Canby wondered how the hell he was going to signal them to stop. In that moment he wished that he'd never gotten himself into this at all, but it was too late to think about that.

It seemed that many of the Indians were breaking away, losing themselves in the darkness. He yelled for men to go after them, but no one paid a bit of attention to him, and he gave up and stretched back down on the ground and let the fight die out of its own spent energy.

For more than thirty minutes riders pounded back and forth, their blood up, shooting at Indians on the ground, Indians running, and at themselves. But it stopped as he'd known it would, and he supposed they had used up all their ammunition, and he felt like swearing at them, but this wasn't the Army; there was no discipline, and losing his temper would only start a fight.

Finally he gathered about him those men he had placed in charge. Six Texans were dead and eleven more were wounded, two of these badly, and no one expected them to live out the night.

He was faced now with things he hadn't even thought of, like medical supplies and a doctor to do what he could. They had nothing, and they made camp there until morning. None of them got much sleep, with the wounded moaning in pain and the bad ones screaming until they died.

Canby thought the damned dawn would never come, but it did, and as soon as it was light, he had fires built and walked around, taking stock of things. The Texans were all through with fighting; you could see it in their eyes. Some of them spoke of mounting up and going home, but Canby wouldn't have it, and they stayed because they didn't want to get into a gunfight with him.

By his estimation, there were seventy dead Indians, and thirty of those had died from gunshot wounds. The others had just died, and when the daylight finally grew stronger, he could see why they had died.

They were covered with running sores, and the word went through the camp like a brush fire: smallpox.

There would have been an instant exodus if the Army had not arrived, the bugler sounding his horn in bright, ripping tones, and the point arriving with the main body coming over a rise.

A young second lieutenant and a sergeant approached first, and Canby was envious of this beardless youth, so efficient, so sure of himself; the lieutenant immediately appraised the situation correctly, ordered the Army to stay out of the camp, but to surround it completely.

The sergeant relayed these orders, and the young officer reported to Colonel Bolton, who, joined by three others, approached Canby. The colonel was in a foul frame of mind; Canby could gather that much from the man's expression.

"Are you the imbecile in charge, Canby?" Bolton asked, stripping off his gloves. "You've done a fine job here. Left alone, the Indians would have camped here and died of smallpox or recovered from it, but now you've scattered them, and it'll spread like the wind." He looked around at the Texans. "And all of these fine citizens have been exposed to it. You've done well, Canby. You ought to get a medal for stupidity."

"How in hell was I to know?" Canby said, then wished he hadn't.

"That's a bright question. In the first place, the Army would have taken care of the Indians, but you wanted it done yesterday. When the hostiles failed to attack us and the surgeon examined a dead Indian we found, he diagnosed smallpox, and we knew what to expect. Then do you know what we did, Mr. Canby? Instead of going off half-cocked, we sat down and thought about it. We started dealing with facts, not emotion, and because we did that, we believe we managed to learn the truth and act wisely. It came to our immediate attention that the hostiles were getting sick, and all at the same time. This could only mean that they contracted the disease at the same time, and since we have been following them for some time now, we reasoned that they got it at the well where the old relay station used to be. One of our doctors is there now taking a sample for examination." He put his hands on his hips and looked around the camp. "You and your men will remain here, under constant guard for three weeks at the least. When my surgeons are satisfied that you are not carrying the disease, you will be permitted to leave. Now I suggest that you take your ragtag outfit away from here, move upstream a hundred yards, and establish a camp. A military detail will burn this one. Any questions?"

"Colonel, we don't have enough rations to last—"

"Oh, I suspected as much," Bolton said. "Canby, you're not bright. Not bright at all."

"You don't have to rub it in."

"I guess I don't. Look around, Canby. Look at their faces. They know when they've been led by a fool."

"Hell, we can all make mistakes!"

"This big?" Bolton asked, then turned to one of his officers without waiting for an answer. "Send in a squad for a wagon and supplies. I want two companies to remain here on guard duty. The rest will form in the morning for the march back."

"Yes, sir."

"Dismissed," Bolton said and turned back to Dan Canby. "For your information, I gave orders before I left to have the farmers moved out of this locality. In fact, I'm cleaning out the county at least until the Indians are on the reservation. The farmers stir the Indians up, and we can't have that, can we?"

"What the hell am I supposed to do about the notes I hold?"

"Why don't you make a fire of them?"

"I'll have to close my bank, colonel!"

"Yes, we'll miss it," Bolton said dryly. "Don't look for sympathy from me. You can always go to farming. After all, you're sitting on a section here and a section there right smack dab in Ben Talon's range. If you know how to plant potatoes, you won't starve."

"You're the funniest thing I've ever heard," Canby snapped. "I lose my shirt and you make jokes." He pawed his mouth out of shape. "And I went and signed a note and put my store up for security so I could pay these men to—" He dropped his hand and fell silent, shaking his head. "How am I going to pay that back now?"

"Now you did get yourself in the hole, didn't you?" Colonel Bolton sighed and pulled on his gloves. "Well, I've got to get a burial detail organized here. You just can't leave dead Indians scattered around the prairie; it isn't tidy."

He walked away and Canby stood there. Several Texans came over, and one said, "If those Indians hadn't of took sick, the Army'd still be chasing its own tail. They've got a helluva nerve telling us what to do. Damned if I'm goin' to stay here under guard."

"The soldiers will shoot if you try to break away," Canby said. "Can't you see that?"

"I can shoot back."

This angered Canby because in this man's hardheaded stubbornness he saw much of his own, and he'd had enough of it. Taking the man by the collar, Canby shook him a little and said, "Don't give me any trouble, Mushy. Don't give anyone else any, either. I can get enough dumb ideas of my own without you coming up with any. Now go on and do as you're told. When a soldier tells you to jump, you just ask how far."

They left him alone, and he sat down on the ground and added it all up and didn't come up with much. There was no doubt in Dan Canby's mind that Amy would take the store; she was that kind of woman, tough enough to stick to her bargains, and she'd see that he stuck to his. The bank was finished; he had no cash reserves, and as soon as word of this got around, depositors would make a run on it, wipe him right out of business.

He had the freight line, and that was all, and right then he was sorry he had that; without it he could just pack up and move someplace else and get another start.

The fact that he could think of such a thing shocked him, angered him anew. Quit, hell! He'd rather take a job sweeping out the saloon. No one was ever going to say that he had quit because he'd been beaten.

He felt better, having decided this, and got up and went over to where the Texans were setting up camp.

13

NONE OF Dan Canby's men returned home until late June. Nearly twenty never came back at all, for some had died in the fighting and the smallpox took the rest.

Colonel Bolton managed to visit the Vale place for a talk with Ben Talon; he related in detail what had happened on the fork of the Red, and this was the first accurate account any of them had, which made it bad news, yet good news, for it ended the worry of many.

Bolton lived with his Indian trouble; they were to the south now, spreading sickness among themselves, and there was little fight in them because they believed their medicine had turned bad and their leaders had lost control.

He also had a new second in command, a Colonel MacKenzie who had a great grasp of situation and a lot of fire and ambition, which gave Bolton some free time to worry about civilians and mule-headed Texans like Dan Canby. Bolton talked and Talon listened, then argued, and Bolton kept talking, and Talon's arguments grew weaker, and finally he agreed that Bolton was right and promised to talk to Fred Early.

Early was sitting on the profits from last year's drive, and he had nine thousand steers on the trail when Talon rode into his yard and joined him on the porch.

"Going to be a hot summer," Early said, pointing to a vacant chair.

"Aren't they all?" He sat down and fanned his face with his hat. "I suppose you heard what happened to Canby?"

Early nodded. "Serves him right. Lucky for him the Indi-

152

ans took the smallpox or his whole bunch might have been wiped out."

"I don't know about that," Ben said. "Canby went off half-cocked, but nobody can say he isn't a good fighter. The Indians' getting sick was just as lucky for the Army as it was for Dan."

Early looked at Talon carefully. "What are you selling, Ben?"

Talon laughed. "Now why would I be selling—"

"You are. I can feel it. And I know I won't like it."

"You're right, Fred." He mopped sweat from his face. "As soon as Dan gets back, the depositors will make a run on his bank. We just can't let that happen."

"I can. I ain't got a dime in there."

"That's what I came to see you about. I'm depositing ten thousand. On my way now and stopped in to see if you'd care to ride in with me and make a deposit." He held up his hand to keep Early from protesting. "Fred, the county needs Canby's bank. However wrongheaded he may have been in the way he went about it, Canby's bank and Canby's gambles and Canby's guts have kept the carpetbagger crew out of our immediate neighborhood. It's either Canby or some Yankee moving in. I'm convinced that we've got to save him."

"You do that and Canby will be right back where he was, selling parcels of land out from under us all."

Ben Talon shook his head. "Not this time, Fred. Before we deposit the money, we'll go into partnership with Canby. You and I can outvote him on any loan. Keep the lid on him."

The notion appealed to Early, and he smiled. "By golly now, I never thought of that. I've always wanted to do a little banking; that's a fact." He heaved his bulk out of the chair. "Ten thousand you say? Give me a few minutes."

Early and Ben Talon rode into town together and immediately saw the crowd in front of the bank. The door was closed, and the shades were drawn, and Talon stopped and spoke to a man. "Canby inside?"

"He's at the hotel. But we're waitin'."

Talon nodded to Early, and they rode on and tied up in front of Canby's store. They crossed the porch and went inside. Amy Leland was behind the counter, and she smiled at them.

"I trust you gentlemen have come in to buy?"

"Came in to see Dan," Talon said. He glanced at one of the clerks. "Go over to the hotel and roll him out."

The man glanced at Amy, and she nodded slightly, and the man peeled off his apron and left. Early turned his head to watch him leave, then said, "You the boss now, Miss Leland?"

"I called my note when it was due," she said. "The place is mine, lock, stock, and barrel. Good merchandise but no bargains. Help yourself to the crackers, though."

"Dan knows this?" Talon asked.

Amy nodded. "He came here first thing. I offered him a job —twelve dollars a week. He stomped out, went to the hotel, and I haven't seen him since."

"See him now," Early said softly and nodded toward the open door. Canby was stalking across the street, and he stomped onto the porch, then stopped just inside the door. He was much thinner, and he wore scars on his face and neck that would never fade.

"Hello, Ben. You want to offer me something, too? Everybody's feeling so damned generous. Amy offered me a job, so let's hear what you have up your sleeve."

"Fred and I came in to make a deposit," Talon said. "Ten thousand apiece. We figure it will be enough to stop a run on your bank."

Dan Canby looked from one to the other. "What's the catch, Ben?"

"Fred and I are full partners. Each with a third of the business."

"And each with a third of the say on how to run it?"

"You catch on fast for a fella who's been sick," Early said. "Take it or leave it. I don't feel like bargaining."

"Neither do I," Canby said wearily. He walked over and leaned against the counter and folded his arms. "My foolishness caused some good men to die. I've put the depositors' money into unsound speculation, and I'm stuck with parcels of land I can't sell. I've lost my store. Frankly, I've lost a lot of pride, and I've come to realize that maybe I wasn't big enough to be a big shot. I believe I need some partners who have more sense than I have."

"All right, it's done then," Talon said, handing his saddle-bag to Fred Early. "Go find the cashier and get him to open the bank. See that everyone in town knows about the deposit. Get those people to go home and leave their money alone."

Early nodded. "Be careful if he starts to horse-trade," he said, nodding toward Canby. Then he went out and down the street.

"He sounds like he doesn't trust me," Canby said.

"Do you blame him? Dan, there's a few things to settle before we go any further. First, sell the freight line. You can find a Yankee speculator who'll pay more than it's worth."

"Why should I? It's making money."

"Damn it, man, we're just saving the bank. We're not pulling you out of anything. You played loose with the depositors' money, and now you've got to dig down in your pocket and make up the difference. The only thing you have left to sell is the freight line. Now about those sections the farmers started to plow up—we may sit down and do some across-the-board trading so that the bank's property is in one lump. We might be able to sell it as a ranch to one of the partners—for instance, you—and have the bank break even on it. But the difference comes out of your pocket."

Canby pursed his lips. "You know, I just thought of something: you turned out to be a better Texan than me, and you're a Yankee."

"You damned fool, I was never in a contest with you!" Talon snapped. Then he blew out his temper in a long breath. "Why in hell don't you get some sense, Dan, and ask Amy to marry you?"

"A man wants to be a success before—" He stopped talking and looked at Amy Leland. "I've wanted to ask you, Amy, but somehow all my ideas got in the way. There ain't much left of me now."

"I was thinking," she said, "that what's left is the only part that's worth anything. You told me once you didn't climb high just to fall, but sometimes we do anyway. Nobody cares how far the drop is, but they watch to see how you get up. I'm watching, Dan. And I don't think you're going to disappoint me."

Dan grinned. "Amy, one thing I always liked about you. You were ready to take a gamble whenever you were pretty sure it would turn out right. But I think you're about to take the biggest one yet."

Ben Talon quietly eased himself out the door.

Wade Everett, a pseudonym for **Will Cook**, is the author of numerous outstanding Western novels as well as historical frontier fiction. He was born in Richmond, Indiana, but was raised by an aunt and uncle in Cambridge, Illinois. He joined the U.S. cavalry at the age of sixteen but was disillusioned because horses were being eliminated through mechanization. He transferred to the U.S. Army Air Force in which he served in the South Pacific during the Second World War. Cook turned to writing in 1951 and contributed a number of outstanding short stories to *Dime Western* and other pulp magazines as well as fiction for major smooth-paper magazines such as *The Saturday Evening Post*. It was in the *Post* that his best-known novel, *Comanche Captives*, was serialized. It was later filmed as *Two Rode Together* (Columbia, 1961) directed by John Ford and starring James Stewart and Richard Widmark. It has now been restored, as was the author's intention, with *The Peacemakers* set in 1870 as the first part and *Comanche Captives* set in 1874 as the second part of a major historical novel titled *Two Rode Together*. Sometimes in his short stories Cook would introduce characters that would later be featured in novels, such as Charlie Boomhauer who first appeared in *Lawmen Die Sudden* in *Big-Book Western* in 1953 and is later to be found in *Badman's Holiday* (1958) and *The Wind River Kid* (1958). Along with his steady productivity, Cook maintained an enviable quality. His novels range widely in time and place, from the Illinois frontier of 1811 to southwest Texas in 1905, but each is peopled with credible and interesting characters whose interactions form the backbone of the narrative. Most of his novels deal with more or less traditional Western themes—range wars, reformed outlaws, cattle rustling, Indian fighting—but there are also romantic novels such as *Sabrina Kane* (1956) and exercises in historical realism such as *Elizabeth, by Name* (1958). Indeed, his fiction is known for its strong heroines. Another common feature is Cook's compassion for his characters who must be able to survive in a wild and violent land. His protagonists make mistakes, hurt people they care for, and sometimes succumb to ignoble impulses, but this all provides an added dimension to the artistry of his work.